Advance praise for *We're All Equal*

"The Rev Dr Susan Jones does great
pondering their relationship with the cl.
and one to come, all "conversations in a coffee shop."

The delight of these books is that serious, significant concepts are clothed in flesh and inscribed on table napkins (when a pen can be found). This delightful style reminds me of the ancient model of the dialogue used from Plato's time.

These participants are, however, much more interesting and livelier than a Plato dialogue or fictional discussion. Their developing stories and wisdom are derived from life experience. Hope in *Wherever you are You are on the Journey* and Charity in *We're All Equally Human* have their personal ups and downs. Susan writes about herself, her reading, coffee and changing perspectives with disarming yet instructive frankness.

Wherever you are explores Hope's journey of considering pastoral ministry, developing her own very inclusive and progressive faith journey. Charity in *We're All Equally Human*, is a young lesbian with a delightful choice of dress and a hard coming out story.

This style works exceptionally well as a light but serious way to explore issues, for these books certainly do explore deep issues, introducing readers to a wide range of concepts (explained by diagrams on the serviettes) and very significant writers.

Fortunate, indeed, are young people who sought and received very sensitive and professional counsel from Susan, and fortunate we are to have books like this, allowing us to explore, ponder, to agree or disagree.

I am especially thrilled by *We're All Equally Human*. A stream of people come to talk to me and I point them to books. This one is so locked into Aotearoa, its stories, and church life, that it will be so useful. I will be recommending it widely to those on the journey of relating faith and sexuality.

On my own journey of coming out, and that of my friends, we have all struggled with theological and biblical issues – probably most writing essays on the subject, and revising them as the journey continues. Susan's book gives tools for proceeding on that journey of theological and biblical reflection. Her words remind me so helpfully that this journey of reflection is one we all need to travel, hopefully with wise and thoughtful people alongside, just as Susan was with Charity."

Professor Peter Lineham, MNZM,
Regional Director of the College of Humanities
at Massey University, Albany.

"Like a mighty tortoise crawls the Church of God, brothers we are treading where we've always trod." This re-imaging of a line in the hymn 'Onward Christian Soldiers' struck an immediate chord. Underlying my reluctance to write a comment about Susan Jones' *We're All Equally Human*, were buried emotions I had thought long dealt with, which Charity's journey revived. Journeying alongside Charity, I was reminded again that the clichéd "coming out" is a life-long journey; one we never grow out of.

As Charity discovers each unexpected, if not surprising, response to her spiritual journey of self-recognition, her coffee conversations reveal rich, insightful explanations. They move across cultural, historical, sociological, and importantly, biblical and theological pathways offering empathetic reassurance. I found myself saying 'yes' and 'yes' and finally 'Hallelujah!'

Susan Jones' *We're all Equally Human* removes the tension that surrounds religious debates on sexuality. This conversation continues on from Susan Jones' *Wherever you are, You are on the Journey*. Both books point to the significance of being "equally human" as our life-long journey.

Yvonne Wilkie,
former Archivist, author in the
history of women in Religion.

We're All Equally Human

Conversations in a Coffee Shop Book 2

Susan Jones

Philip Garside Publishing Ltd.

Email Susan at: jones.rs@xtra.co.nz
Follow her on: www.jonessmblog.wordpress.com

Paperback International edition
ISBN 9781991027016

Also available
New Zealand paperback: ISBN 9781988572970
Paperback print-on-demand USA: ISBN 9798439964321
PDF: ISBN 9781988572987
ePub: ISBN 9781988572994
Kindle/Mobi: ISBN 9781991027009

Philip Garside Publishing Ltd
PO Box 17160
Wellington 6147
New Zealand
books@pgpl.co.nz — www.pgpl.co.nz

Cover photograph:
Rainbow coloured coffee mug on table
ID 144663569 © Richracer | Dreamstime.com

Coffee cups line art:
Rosemary Garside

Contents

Introduction

I trained for ministry in the 1990s. Around that time, in my corner of the world, that world changed. Just before I entered training, a male ministry student was 'outed' by a fellow student as being gay. This became the subject of a special national gathering in our denomination.

Thus began a long debate in the church I belonged to, on whether elders and ministers in the church could be in gay relationships. From about 1991, for two decades, this specific debate threatened to and sometimes did take over the annual church conferences, other programmes being subsequently squeezed for time, space, and attention.

1991 was my first attendance at such a gathering. I hadn't yet begun ministry training. It was a baptism by fire. I watched, cried, spoke emotionally from the heart, suffered, dissented, and learned.

As time went by, I became one of those bringing overtures for debate. Speaking times got trimmed to contain all business within the time available. It was less and less possible to address the issue substantively in the three and five minutes allowed to speakers. We persisted, however, inevitably talking past each other. Bans and restrictions were applied, rescinded, and applied again. Both sides of the argument felt their liberty of conscience, enshrined in 19th century church documents, was threatened.

In contrast to those truncated debate speeches, I consider it a privilege that in this book I am able to integrate ideas, arguments, knowledge, and experience in a longer span than a three-minute speech. The book seeks to highlight the underlying reasons why this debate is especially heated and so thoroughly defended within a national church as it transitions from the 20th to 21st centuries.

My conversation partner in the coffee shop, Charity, is a representative character. She combines several aspects of many young members of the rainbow and straight communities with whom I've talked in coffee shops from time to time during my ministry. This book is therefore most accurately described as a non-fiction novel. Its content is real.

Some of it is approximately autobiographical, though conversations and characters have been woven together imaginatively.

Charity is aptly named. Despite the hurt and frustration which I and others have experienced in this debate, this book comes with love. It seeks to be respectful to all sides. We all grow up in different settings with different experiences. We see life and faith in varied ways. We inhabit diverse stages of faith. Our experience of people is narrow, wider, or vast. That varied experience influences how we see individuals and communities other than our own. Had I been brought up differently, I would not be the person I am now.

If you are someone whom this debate has hurt, I hope you find healing and understanding as well as information within these pages.

If you have picked up this book and find yourself opposed to its stance, I ask that you read with an open mind.

Whoever you are and wherever you are, we are all on the journey to being fully human.

For many, this debate is an integral part of our journey in this time and place. For many it is an integral part of their lives and very being. For others it is an integral part of their belief system and their faith walk.

Please pay attention to what your inner heart says to you as you read.

Please walk this path in love.

Above all, please listen for the 'unforced rhythms of grace.'[1]

Susan
March 2022

Dedicated to Frances Porter
whose banner will march on

Trigger and Content Warnings

A young lesbian woman who read a draft of this book suggested trigger warnings might be helpful in some chapters, especially for when suicide and other difficult topics are mentioned.

I hate that the world is such that this topic (as it is played out in my church at the moment) would distress people to this extent. I am very happy however, to include a warning system for readers who might find some sections confronting.

Seeing a warning, you may then choose to read on with caution, avoid a chapter altogether for ever, or, after reading the rest of the book come back when you are in a good space, able to endure the confronting material in a different way.

Whichever is your choice, look after yourself, be gentle, do not allow yourself to be retraumatised.

Understanding warnings

Trigger and content warnings give advance notice of upcoming sensitive content or imagery that may affect you negatively. I want to avoid anyone having a panic attack, or worse.

An advance warning puts the choice to read or not to read into your hands if you have had traumatic experiences. Our aim in using warnings is to create a safe space, where those who have suffered the trauma can decide how or if they will engage.

Content warnings

These alert you the reader to something which might upset you, e.g. in this book, that might be graphic biblical events or accounts of church decisions which exclude people.

Trigger warnings

These are used to prevent anyone with past trauma being exposed to a passage which might cause a physical and/or mental reaction, e.g. sexual violence.

At the beginning of a chapter which needs a warning, there will be an abbreviation **CW** or **TW** with two slashes **CW//** or **TW//**. Relevant keywords are then added, e.g. "**CW //** difficult church decisions or **TW //** sexual violence."

Because each chapter has a range of content, we have then added page number(s) so you can be assured it's safe to read other parts of the chapter if you wish. If this bothers you, of course, skip the whole chapter if you wish.

Let me add that I am very, very sorry previous trauma in your life might re-affect you as you read this book. It is a book intended for healing and I hope you can find some of that here.

As a member of the church about which I am writing, I apologise for the ways this debate has hurt or traumatised you further. I am ashamed that people calling themselves Christian can conduct themselves in such a way that members of the rainbow community feel abused, unwanted, and rejected. I am sorry.

I hope you can realise, despite all that noise, that you are loved, no matter who and what you are.

Specific warnings in this book

1. Homophobia, transphobia, and sexism (any kind of discrimination).

   Unfortunately, the content of the whole book needs to revolve around 'homophobia, transphobia, and sexism (any kind of discrimination)'. It may be a difficult read for many people, rainbow community members, straight church members, partners, spouses, parents, and friends. In that sense the whole book needs to come with a 'content warning'. If we do not read widely and thoroughly, however, even views with which we disagree, then we do not grow. I wish you well with this challenge.

Other warnings employed in different chapters of this book include:

2. Death by violence
3. Sexual violence / rape
4. Paedophilia
5. Violence / murder
6. Suicide
7. Talk of dysphoria, body image and appearance
8. Difficult church decisions

If you are triggered by anything in this book and need support, Appendix Two has resources and numbers for helplines which can be accessed in New Zealand.

Above all, let me remind you: "Love surrounds you every moment of everyday."

Susan

1 – Encounter

The church hall is a hive of activity. The Youth Expo we're hosting is humming. All around the space, stalls with brightly coloured bunting are crowded with customers and enquirers.

We'd planned a mix of stalls. Some, interspersed with others around the hall, offer resources and information which young people might need in the city. Others are food stalls or sell T-shirts, second-hand clothing, and fair trade goods. Two other stalls are local start-ups, one selling environmentally friendly re-usable coffee cups and water bottles while the other sells small ornaments and furniture made from recycled plastic.

"Over here!" My head swivels to the left.

Charity Brown is staffing the Young Rainbows stall, its multi-coloured bunting making a bright splash in front of the stage. The stall is offering a mix of general rainbow information and other resources produced by our church. I'd run off some of my own reflections given in church during Pride Month. There's a poetry book by a group of young rainbow community members and some 'zines' with the general title, *Being gay and ....* We had a few titles we'd managed to get together for the occasion: *Being gay and Christian, Being gay and spiritual, Being gay having left the church, Being gay and reading the Bible.* It'd been interesting working with the small group of rainbow young people in our church to see what questions they wanted answering in the zines. It was illuminating to hear the questions they were being asked by their gay friends who didn't go to church.

Beaming at me, Charity waves me over. It is a good occasion for her to wear her floppy rainbow-sequinned cap jammed on her auburn curls. I admire her T-shirt which lists, in appropriate colours; the words 'purple grapes, blueberries, green apples, yellow cherries, oranges and red currants.'

"Nice shirt," I greet her, "very subtle."

Charity looks down at herself and grins. "My brother gave me this when I came out to the family," she says proudly.

She and her twin brother are close, and his positive reaction had meant a lot to her.

It wasn't long since Charity came out to her parents. In the strange (to a straight person) way of the rainbow community, people could be out in some situations but not to other groups of people they knew. Charity had been out at university for a year or more. She'd come out around our church in the last six months. Her parents were almost the last people she told. She'd found to her relief they were more accepting than she thought they would be. They'd been putting two and two together and making a fairly accurate four. I admired them for how they'd dealt with their understandable grief, that the big hetero wedding and heaps of grandchildren they'd imagined might not now happen in quite the same way, or at all. They'd dealt with their personal grief separately from encouraging and supporting Charity, so she wasn't burdened with their issues.

Charity's parents were local politicians. Leaning towards green politics, her father and mother were on the local regional council and the city council respectively. I don't think, in her anxiety about coming out, Charity had realised how many rainbow members were in the Green Party and how familiar her parents were with gay issues. Since her family had lived in quite a remote area of the country during her school years, Charity had gone to boarding school. Perhaps she had not seen her parent's own maturing in relation to rainbow issues. Now they lived nearer to the university where she was studying, she saw them more often.

"We're getting a lot of interest," Charity enthuses. "The zines are flying off the table. Those illustrations Tom did are really eye catching. Also, the size is good. I've seen a few being shoved in jeans pockets while the person moves quickly on."

Her green eyes sparkle. Charity is a good person for such a stall. Extroverted, she loves interacting with people, but having been closeted herself for a long time, she knows when to engage and when to let people be.

"Looking forward to next week?" I ask after checking no one else was coming up to the table right now. Charity was attending our church's national conference as a youth representative. It would be her first experience of such a meeting. I wondered how she would find it.

"Yeeees," says Charity cautiously. "I've heard from others who've been and I'm not sure how I will go if it gets very heated. But there are interesting discussions planned in the environmental area, so I'll enjoy that. I'm looking forward to the guest speaker too."

"Yes!" I respond.

We had all been surprised that a relatively young and creative presenter had been chosen to deliver the keynote addresses. I envied Charity having the chance to hear the presentations live, though podcasts would be released afterwards.

"Need a coffee?" I ask.

I'd been going round the room getting coffees for the stall holders from the coffee truck outside. Stall holding could be a long thirsty job.

"Yes please! Chai latte with cinnamon on top."

"Your wish is my command," I joke moving out into the crowded middle of the hall.

Our aim of resourcing young people and offering free and low-cost resources seems to be working. We had more attending this year than last, when we'd inaugurated the two-day Expo. Perhaps we could add a food pantry next year since the Veggie Coop's stall was doing a roaring trade. Not only were they selling vegetables off their stall today, but quite a few student flats were signing up for their weekly deliveries. It was a cheap way to get lots of good quality vegetables. Their cooking classes were filling up fast too. Some of the students needed to learn how to cook vegetables quickly and well.

Back at Charity's stall, she is engaged in a deep conversation with a young student with lots of piercings and a black T shirt that proclaims, "Some people are gay, get over it!" I put Charity's chai latte down in front of her, offer my own takeaway Americano to the student and leave them to it.

I hope Charity's experiences the next week wouldn't be too challenging. Our church could be unconsciously cruel in the way it conducts debates on what had become known as "the gay issue."

I look up and see Charity's girlfriend Katy coming into the hall. It embarrassed me that people like Katy, who'd exited the church after an abusive fundamentalist upbringing, should see a so-called broader church being so draconian in its moral judgments. It certainly didn't encourage Katy, and many others, to dip their toes back into organised church waters any time soon. I sigh inwardly, then smile at Katy.

"Hi Katy, come to take her away?" I ask.

Katy grins at me from under her heavy straight black fringe. "Oh! Hi! Yep, she's been here all afternoon and we have a date with a pizza and a movie," she replies.

"Sounds great! Her relief has just arrived, I think," I say as I see Tom and his partner Blake approaching the stall. "Take her away and romance her," I suggest.

Surprised, Katy gives me a cautious look. She still can't get used to a minister approving of gay relationships. It hadn't been her experience in the past. "Yeah," she says, warily.

I smile. Katy would get used to our inclusive attitude here. It would take time. I hope Charity's experiences next week, won't affect Katy's and her trust levels too badly, but I wasn't too sure. Intending to do the right thing, the church frequently didn't get it right in the end.

2 – How we decide what is good

I wait in *The Cup* for Charity to arrive, sitting in line with the door so I can keep an eye out for her bright red curly head of hair floating behind her as she dashes from point A to point B. Mostly, she's a ball of energy, but I wonder how she will be today.

The Cup offers its usual warm welcome, delicious smells of coffee and freshly baked rolls. Located just across the busy city street from the church where I work, it's close both for me, and to Charity's flat a block away.

Charity's attended the same church fairly regularly in the last couple of years. She's part of the young adults group, *Sunday Stuff,* whose chaotic and crazy programme creates community among a mix of gen Y and Z students, straight, gay, trans and non-binary, queer and questioning. *The Cup* is a favourite place for them to gather afterwards. Its small, noisy shop fronting the street balanced by a quiet courtyard out the back, with its mural of hanging plants, has an Italian ambiance. In good weather, *Sunday Stuff* students gather round the big table in the middle of the courtyard, changing the world tens of times over in animated discussion.

Charity had phoned in distress this morning after returning from attending our church's national conference. She's new to our denomination's life. Her parents' church going days are in the past, but Charity's begun to explore spirituality on her own account. She came to one of our Pride Week services three years ago, then the next year, kept on coming after Pride Week was over.

I had thought before Charity went to conference that she would find it an eye opener. I was ashamed our Church had been fighting over how it should regard homosexuality especially in relation to elders and ministers for some decades now. Full on, for about 30 years in fact.

I'd attended national church conferences off and on for those 30 years, both as an elder, and, after I'd trained, as a parish minister. I'd been continually upset at the ongoing rejection of a humane way of treating all people. The local group which worked towards reconciling differences between straight and gay communities had needed to re-group more than once after alienating decisions had been made. I led one of their alternative worship services locally some years ago. The liturgy I had written, and other liturgy I adapted from other writers, expressed our pain. Being together in solidarity had helped too.[2] I am still shocked, however, at how thoroughly I'd been able to tuck it all away after the trauma of each gathering was over. It's like a compartment of my brain is labelled "I thought that would happen, but the time will come." Compartmentalising has become habitual. Over the years it's been a coping mechanism. I've come to see however, that it isn't good for me to split it all off like that.

Charity doesn't have even that experience. She can't take comfort from any of her own memories that voting numbers are slowly, ever so slowly, edging towards acceptance of gay women and men as ordained leaders and ministers. Nor that voting against the ban on ministers conducting same sex marriages is getting even closer to succeeding. She'd known greater acceptance of the rainbow community in the sector of New Zealand society which she inhabits. Church attitudes are becoming embarrassingly archaic. Unfortunately, like the 'Trump effect,'[3] public rejection of same sex orientation by churches such as ours allows secular homophobes to see the rainbow community as fair targets for verbal and physical violence.

I don't have all the answers. I have no personal experience of what it's like to face the hurtful reactions rainbow community members get from both church and society. Each time I talk with a Charity or her male equivalent, like Tom and Blake, gay guys in the choir at our church, I learn a bit more. I'm also constantly learning more of the myriad of ways heteros like me can put our foot in our mouth without realising why and how we'd done it. I did know I wanted to be an ally, a friend, and an unconditional supporter. If that caused tension with my role as minister in an institutional church, so be it. Love and compassion were more important than rules.

It took 41 years from the first official suggestion to final reality for women to be accepted as ministers in my denomination. I sigh wearily. 11 years to go. Were we only that far through this current argument? A parody of 'Onward Christian Soldiers' springs into my mind. It replaces the words "Like a mighty army moves the church of God, brother we are treading where the saints have trod" with

"Like a mighty tortoise crawls the Church of God, brothers we are treading where we've always trod." Relevant, I think, to this debate in the church currently. Also, the war-like metaphor unfortunately was all too apt sometimes for the tone of the debate. But all great changes take time.

The door to *The Cup* opens and Charity, glorious green eyes dull and red-rimmed, comes in on an early summer breeze. I move towards her, ducking my head under the huge floppy brim of her summery hat and we hug, comforting each other.

"Double shot trim flat white?" I ask, finally pulling away.

"Yes please! I need the caffeine!" replies Charity fumbling in her pocket for a tissue. She goes quickly to a table hidden in the far corner of the courtyard, keeping her hat on. With a stabbing sensation in my heart, I realise she's trying to hide her distress from the other customers. I order and pay.

Once we settle, I look her in the eye. "Tough time away?" I ask with a wry twist to my mouth.

"Oh boy! Tough! How can Christians be so rejecting! And make such huge assumptions! I felt like they're expecting gay ministers to run an orgy every week in the manse! Or that all gay Christians are hopelessly promiscuous! I might not mind their ignorance about gays, but a lot of my heterosexual friends are exactly that, so how can they preach as if being heterosexual makes you perfect? My straight friends are having one-night stands all over the place. What's more, according to the news, not all hetero church leaders are known for sexual self-restraint! What's that saying? 'Those living in glasshouses shouldn't throw stones'?"

I nod. Charity is expressing what I had said and thought on many similar occasions. I figure she needs to let off more steam, so keep listening.

"It was like the two sides to the debate were talking past each other. The conservative speakers didn't seem to be interested in equity or justice. They kept on talking about the Bible forbidding 'it'! I thought God was a God of love. I thought Christians were meant to welcome all. I thought forgiveness was the thing in Christianity."

"The statement that really got in my throat was that hoary old 'we love the sinner but hate the sin.'" Charity punctuates the remark with air quotes. "What's with that! The way they said it you could tell they thought they'd made things better, not knowing they'd just made them worse!"

Our drinks arrive and we both take sips of the still-too-hot but stimulating coffee. We simultaneously sigh with relief and pleasure and grin at each other.

"You've hit several nails on the head there all at once," I say. "Will we take them one by one?"

Charity smiles tremulously. "That might be a good idea. I've been raging out loud and inside ever since I got back. Now it's all going round and round in my head in a hopeless, angry muddle. Katy has been great, but she wasn't there. She gets madder than I do since she's given up on church completely and doesn't think I should give it the time of day. I have to say, it's times like this when it's a comfort having the love of a good woman."

"Well done, Katy!" I exclaimed. I like Charity's girlfriend. The physical opposite to Charity, petite with straight black hair, Katy is a confident, assertive young woman, strong in spirited debate and gentle in relationships.

"Let me add to Katy's demonstration of true love by reminding you that you are loved by God too, whoever you are and whatever you have done," I said using a phrase Charity would know well from the liturgy I use in church. Charity nods slowly, tears welling up again, different tears from those she'd shed when she arrived. Less angry.

"You were baptised as an infant, right?" She nods.

"Well, no one knew at that point what kind of person you would turn out to be. Yet, the Church sanctioned you being baptised as an outward sign of God's grace shown to you. That you turned out to be a feisty young gay woman is a bonus!"

We chuckle quietly. I find it good too to be reminded of what grace offers human beings. As a straight supporter of gays' position in the church I also often feel rejected by right-wing conservative Christians. I come away from most church conferences feeling bruised and battered, friendless and judged. I too had noticed some I knew well chose not to talk with me in the breaks at our national gatherings. Sometimes I had the uncomfortable feeling groups of more conservative ministers were talking about me, especially after a debate in which I had spoken up.

Charity takes another sip of her flat white. She is beginning to relax a little.

"Let's look at the 'hate the sin' thing," I suggest. "If those who say this really thought it through, they would realise for homosexuals as well as heterosexuals, sexuality is part of the whole of our lives. It's more than a separate act we do in the bedroom. We live in and embrace the world all the time as the whole people we are. A gay woman reacts to trees and political news and handbags and housing differently from the way a straight woman does. Our sexuality isn't something we can cut out or cut off, or on which we can lock the door and throw away the key. It's impossible to separate ourselves from our actions. We are one and the same, integrated beings through and through."

"Imagine if you said to a straight person, I hate that you have heterosexual intercourse, but I love you as a person, how insulted they would be?" added Charity, eyes flashing green fire.

"Indeed. You know the confectionery called Rock which they have in England?"

"Yep," replies Charity looking a little puzzled but intrigued.

"Well, the name of the town where it's made goes through the bar from beginning to end. If it's from Blackpool (where my Mum was born), at every point where you break the stick of rock, you'll find the word 'Blackpool.' It's really cool, though terrible for your teeth."

"That's what I'm talking about – wherever I encounter a gay person in their life they will be being their own gay self, not just when they're making out."

Charity's grin spreads slowly over her face. I'm glad to see it.

"That's right!" she exclaims. "I'm gay through and through, just like they are straight through and through. That's why the huge concession they thought they were making didn't feel good to me. They were saying, 'you're OK if you just don't do this bit' when all of me is gay, just like all of them is straight, not just the sexy behaviour."

"Exactly. And that's not even beginning to deal with the fact that when you really study scripture with an open mind, it doesn't say that a mutual, loving gay relationship is sinful. The so-called 'sinner' part is questionable as is the so-called 'sin' part. We can get into that in more detail down the track."

Charity nods, taking off her floppy hat and running her fingers through her long wavy hair. The gesture seems symbolic, as if she's regaining her sense of worth and doesn't need to hide away from the world anymore. I can see even the conversation so far, brief as it's been, is lessening her confusion and justifiable anger, so I continue.

"Then, I think you said you felt the two sides of this debate didn't care what the other thought? What did you say? 'They were talking past each other.' That's very perceptive. I didn't start noticing that until I'd been to about five or six national gatherings, coming home each time feeling rejected and ignored."

I continue, "one thing to remember is that people on both sides of this argument are not thinking and reacting reasonably. They're acting out of emotions and later finding reasons to support the emotional 'decisions' they're making. That's usual for all arguments. This argument is happening in the context of spirituality and the church, both very significant arenas of people's lives, so it provokes extra-large emotional reactions at both ends of the spectrum. It follows that arguments on both sides need to appeal to emotions as well as to logic."

"Is that written down anywhere?" asks Charity, "I'd love to read more about that."

"Yes, it's in Jonathan Haidt's book *The Righteous Mind*.[4] You might find his ideas more accessible in his TED talks.[5] Perhaps use them as an introduction first."

I reach for a table napkin and fumble for a pen in my (as always) over-full handbag. This habit of losing my pen has driven me wild over the years. I finally grab one proclaiming the merits of a certain type of car tyre (don't know where I picked that up!). Finally, I write down Jonathan's name and the title of the book.

"He also came up with another point which helped my understanding of this debate. He warns liberal people that writing off conservative people as just dumb is a mistake. They are emoting and thinking as hard about this topic as liberals do. They just do it from different perspectives."

"Hmmm!!" says Charity.

Her exclamation sounds a little sceptical, so I hurry on…

"Haidt argues there are about six or seven principles which we all use at different times to argue a moral point. Both progressive and conservative people think all these principles are important, but they emphasise different ones. You were talking about equity and justice as important points to be made in the debate, right?"

Charity nods, face absorbed, sipping her coffee absent-mindedly.

"Actually, conservative people think those values are important in making moral decisions too, but they value more highly, 'authority,' 'loyalty' and 'sanctity or purity.'

Charity grimaces. "Don't those kinds of values prop up racism, sexism and homophobia? I don't think I would trust authority, loyalty and sanctity as reasons for a moral judgement."

"Exactly Haidt's point. That doesn't mean as a liberal person you would never value sanctity/purity. It means you'd use it as a moral foundational value only when you're sure it's not being used to oppress a group or person. But what you just said does mean you're not as likely to use sanctity/purity as an argument in a debate like this one."

Charity nods slowly, her face thoughtful.

"What role do you think the value of sanctity/purity played in the debate you were just part of?" I ask.

She thinks hard, brow furrowed. Charity is intelligent, majoring in psychology. She'll get the answer quickly. Sure enough, her face soon lights up.

"The promiscuity arguments. They were worried about the purity of the manse and the sanctity of marriage."

"Exactly. Now, let's think of another of those values. What was brought into the conservative's arguments when they used the concept of loyalty in making a moral choice?"

Charity's brow knits again as she thinks, absent-mindedly tucking a stray strand of hair behind her ear as she ponders. This one is harder. She replies slowly.

"People were saying that the Church had never condoned homosexuality and that this debate was over a moral idea in which the church should lead society. They also quoted other reformed churches overseas who had the same kinds of rules, excluding gays."

"That's right." I agree. "They were looking around at people who think and theologise like them. They want to align themselves with that group. It doesn't help here in New Zealand when there's a very loud right-wing lobby in the States grabbing headlines quite often on sexual orientation issues. Conservatives in New Zealand don't want to be out of step with that group since they think the same on a lot of other issues."

I continue, "what was brought into conservative arguments when they used the value of authority in making a moral choice?"

Again, Charity frowns in concentration, teeth biting into her bottom lip. Slowly, I see the connection being made.

"The Bible. For them, the Bible is the ultimate authority. That's why they call it God's Word. That's why they quote the Bible so often and so precisely. I get it now. It's a major authority."

"You've got it. Haidt proposed six values which form the foundations for anyone's moral theory." I reach for the napkin and write in a column six pairs of opposites, *Care / Harm, Fairness & Justice / Cheating, Loyalty / Betrayal, Authority / Rebellion, Sanctity / Impurity, Liberty / Oppression.*

"We could describe them in questions." I go down the list adding a question for each pair of words.

1. Care / Harm — Who is being harmed and how?
2. Fairness & Justice / Cheating — How just is this for everyone? Who's losing out?
3. Loyalty / Betrayal — Who is 'in' and who is 'out'?
4. Authority / Rebellion — What authority are we following or disobeying?
5. Sanctity / Impurity — What standards of behaviour do we follow?
6. Liberty / Oppression — Who is free? Who is being oppressed?

"Which of these would you say the liberals in the debate were using to make their points?"

Charity tilts her head to look at the list. Her finger moves down the words.

"'Care/harm' – they were arguing that gays and lesbians would be put off the church and their families hurt by the rejection. Some even quoted high suicide rates among gay Christians."

"Yes," I nod. "Researchers in the States found, I quote, 'Although religiosity is generally tied to reduced suicide risk, the opposite may be true for some young lesbian, gay and questioning adults.' They looked at more than 21,000 college students and found 'greater religious feeling and engagement was tied to increased risk of suicidal thoughts and actions for participants who identified as LGBQ.' It's criminal. I remember that article well. The title was 'Religious faith linked to suicidal behaviour in LGBQ adults.' What a thing to read as you're scrolling through the internet."[6]

"Also, a 2011 New Zealand study found that same sex attracted or bisexual young people were more likely to become depressed and that mental health support was needed urgently for that group of young people."[7]

"Indeed!" exclaims Charity. "Both those studies sound depressing but at least they have been done."

"I remember more now," she continues. "At the conference another argument the liberals used was 'Justice/cheating.' They argued excluding LGBTQI Christians from ordained positions was unfair, especially as heterosexual elders and ministers are sometimes known to betray their marriage vows." Her finger keeps moving down the list. "And this one too, 'Liberty/oppression'. They saw it as a human rights and freedom issue. They argued gays were being oppressed by this rejection."

"You're right. Yet, Haidt argues that a conservative might, at times, also argue from those values. Some research into how this works came up with a graph like this."

I turn the napkin over and roughly sketch an approximation of Haidt's diagram.

"This research used purity for the concept of sanctity and didn't test for liberty/oppression."

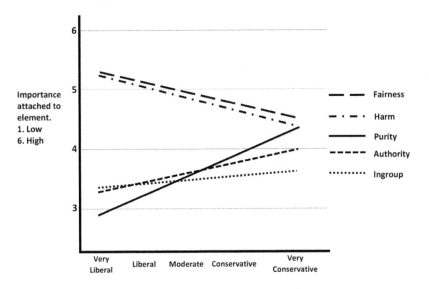

Values preferred by liberals and conservatives

"You can see that values relating to harm and fairness are highly important for very liberal people, while loyalty, authority and purity are not as important."

"For the very conservative person, however, these three values score more highly. For very conservative people harm and fairness are quite highly regarded arguments too. It would be good to know what kind of harm and what kind of fairness they were thinking of. Harm to whom and fairness for what group?"

"No wonder we were talking past each other!" breathes Charity, poring over the diagram, tracing the lines with her fingers.

"Yes. Given Haidt's analysis, it seems inevitable that happens. It would be good homework for all liberals to see if they could mount three arguments in favour of ordination of LGBTQI Christians in the church, using authority, sanctity/purity and loyalty/ingroup as their basis."

"Why don't I try that?" asks Charity, her face lighting up with the idea. "I'll look at each value one at a time and see if I can come up with a pro-argument aligned with each."

"Great! We can talk about how you are getting on next time," I reply. "Now, how's Psych going at the moment?"

We fall into study-talk until Charity looks at her watch and declares she needs to leave to meet Katy at the movie theatre for the Gay Film Festival re-run of *Pride*.[8]

"That's a neat movie. You'll enjoy that. A friend of mine walked in the real-life Gay Pride Parade they show at the end. I won't tell you the rest of that story until you've seen it."

When we part at the door, Charity is looking less emotional and beaten.

What a gruelling time young gay Christians experience. Not only are they adjusting to coming out to friends and family with what might be, for the friends and family, a surprising 'new' sexual orientation. At the same time, they are in a church claiming to be a loving faith community, but where, suddenly, they need to defend themselves.

It is depressing and alienating to find your very self is unacceptable to others.

3 – In the group, out of the group, in no group

"I'm stumped," says Charity plopping herself down in the booth at *The Cup*, tugging off her cool sequinned rainbow beret, characteristically running hands through her auburn hair, then tossing that hair back over her shoulders.

"I've racked my brains to think of how I could make a loyalty or ingroup argument about including LGBTQI people which was palatable to conservatives."

It's a warm summer day. I've escaped my stifling office, taking refuge in the cool courtyard to work on the reflection for Sunday. I move my laptop from the centre of the table and focus on her exasperated face, pushing the iced coffee I'd taken the liberty of ordering for her across the table.

"I can see why liberals don't use this basis for moral argument very often," she continues. "Loyalty and ingroup arguments lead to exclusivism. It could be argued they're the underlying basis of the worst of our colonial attitudes. You know, the attitude that only the colonisers are worthy of good treatment. That's the kind of attitude which has oppressed indigenous peoples for centuries."

"It's certainly a strange way of thinking for those brought up in a liberal atmosphere in their family or church," I say. "My church of origin was conservative. I only realised in later years that it was fundamentalist in its basic orientation. We were certainly living in a Baptist bubble."

"What is fundamentalism really about?" asks Charity. "I kind of think of it as a group of people who have very black and white views on almost everything. Isn't fundamentalism the kind of belief that underlies cults and sects?"

"I looked fundamentalism up the other day and found this in the online Britannica." I swivel my laptop around and after clicking through a few pages show Charity what had come up under "Christian fundamentalism."

> … fundamentalists affirmed a core of Christian beliefs that included the historical accuracy of the Bible, the imminent and physical Second Coming of Jesus Christ, and Christ's Virgin

Birth, Resurrection and Atonement. Fundamentalism became a significant phenomenon in the early 20th century and remained an influential movement in American society into the 21st century.[9]

"Oh," says Charity softly as she takes in the words. "It's not just black and white thinking generally, it's also a set of beliefs connected with definite topics."

"Yes," I reply. "Twelve small volumes of essays about 'the fundamentals' were printed in Chicago in the early 20th century. They reaffirmed what were thought of as the fundamentals of which no proper believing Christian should lose sight. The essays were a response to the rise of Darwinism and what fundamentalists see as the evils of evolution."

Charity looks again at the laptop. "I guess people who liked black and white thinking would like these particular doctrines being definitively confirmed. By the way, I like that black and white pattern on your top. Are you sure you're not a closet fundamentalist? Or did you dress especially for the occasion?"

I laugh. Charity frequently notices what people wear, but this morning I had grabbed the coolest thing I could find in the wardrobe. "No fashion pun intended," I reply, then continue.

"I agree about the definition of ideas which you're talking about. Britannica says these beliefs are consistent with 'traditional Christian doctrines concerning biblical interpretation, the mission of Jesus Christ, and the role of the church in society.'"

"What doctrines concerning biblical interpretation do they mean?" asks Charity, pointing to the phrase.

"That includes the inerrancy of Scripture, that it was inspired by God, so contains God's very words to us and that the Bible should be interpreted literally. At least, that is the fundamentalist view of it."

"Wow," says Charity, obviously still thinking hard. "This reminds me of Susie, a friend at school. She was in a fundamentalist church. She wasn't allowed to go to the school dances, her family was teetotal, and I remember her brother, Gareth, who was gay, left home as soon as he could. I'm not sure whether he ever came back. Her mother was very anti-abortion as well, went to all the protests."

"That does sound like the type of behaviour that goes with fundamentalism. Do you know what happened to Gareth? And to Susie?"

"Well, Gareth was lucky, I suppose. He left home to study dentistry and then went overseas. I think he ended up treating quite important people in London, had a partner and did very well for himself. I doubt whether he attended church ever again though. I don't know whether his parents ever worked it all out or not. They may have, and just not been prepared to talk about it to their church friends, even my Mum who was Susie's Mum's best friend. Susie? She married, home schooled her kids and is a teacher's aide in a country school near where her husband Rob farms. They are still dedicated church people. We don't have much in common these days."

"Perhaps when you're thinking of an argument which involves loyalty to the ingroup, you might think of talking with Susie. She sounds like the kind of person to whom you might direct this kind of conversation."

"Mmm," murmurs Charity. "That's a thought."

"I was a Susie. I remember the attitudes I was brought up with. They became second nature for me for a while. Looking back, I realise now I was trained quite subtly to make sure I mixed most of my time with Christians. Keeping going to church when I was a university student was important. I even wore a hat and gloves and my best outfit to go to church when all the other uni students were spending Sunday mornings in their jeans in the hostel common room, reading the Sunday papers. I felt a kind of basic mistrust for people who drank, went out dancing, didn't attend church or slept with their boyfriends. Perhaps a little envy as well! I 'knew' I shouldn't mix with people who were different from who I was."

"Did that include gay people too?"

"In our church homosexuality was hardly mentioned. But, you know, only recently, from various comments and signs, I realise probably at least five young people, around our church when I was a teenager, later came out. I don't know what their experience was like growing up in our church. They weren't openly vilified partly because the adults were ignorant about LGBTQI issues. On the other hand, because their orientation was never visible either, they had no role models of how to be Christian and gay at the same time.

"Wasn't going to university and mixing with a wider group of students a bit of a culture shock for you?" asks Charity, her eyes sparkling with curiosity.

"It was a big shock! How to handle myself at parties and dances where there was alcohol was a nightmare of social embarrassment and plain fear. It was my second year that I really got to know a diverse group of girls in my hostel, and we roomed near each other. Some were sleeping with boyfriends in the same hostel who were keen on partying. Later, when we all went flatting, I wanted to flat with the 'cool' group, (four out of the seven of us). They said I wouldn't fit in. They were right! I ended up flatting with two quieter girls from families which had some connection with church but not a lot. Two others joined us, one a local minister's daughter. She was keen to kick over the traces though, so as a flat we experienced what I came to realise was the usual scenario of relationships starting and crashing. I played a Mother Confessor role from the side-lines!"

"Gosh," responds Charity who'd been listening, wide eyed. "What an adjustment. That gives me a bit of an idea of how the 'ingroup' thing works for conservative Christians. It sounds a little like political affiliation in our household. Mum and Dad have always been Green Party supporters and they severely criticise other political parties. If I fell in love with a woman who was a right-wing ACT party supporter, I don't know how that would be received," she laughed. "It's just as well Katy's a keen environmentalist!"

"By the way," I ask. "Talking of Katy, how was the movie you saw last week?"

"It was great! This small group of gays and lesbians in London decide to collect for the British miner's strike in the 1980s. The trouble comes when they try to find a Welsh village which will accept their donations. The whole movie is a kind of awkward getting-to-know-you scenario between the rainbow group and the miner's side."

"A real example of two in groups not knowing much about each other?"

Charity thought for a minute, then her face lit up. "Yes! Of course, I didn't put it together till you mentioned it. They were two definite ingroups each thinking the other was 'out.' What was that you said about your friend walking in the Parade which you see at the end of the movie?"

"Clare? She lived in London at the time. In fact, she knows that bookshop you saw in the movie well. She was living in London just after she'd come out to her parents, and it hadn't gone well. Her Dad was particularly macho. He'd been in the army and had spent time as a coal miner himself. When the Gay Pride parade came along, Clare marched in it. You saw in the movie that the miners turned up to support it? Well, when she was talking on the phone to her Mum about it all, her Dad came on the phone and said something like "This gay thing can't be too bad if the miners support it!"

Charity and I laughed till we cried at the irony. "So exactly what we're talking about," Charity exclaimed when she could find the breath to speak. "If a person finds that a group they already trust supports something they don't, it can persuade them. Oh my. How cool." She takes a breath and dabs her eyes.

"What led to your change from that ingroup fundamentalism to now?"

"Education would be one way. My early biblical studies papers opened my eyes to more varied ways of interpreting Scripture."

I think for a moment and continue. "Other ways would be the reality of meeting and getting to know people unlike me. It started with those girls in the hostel. I liked them as friends. When they started acting in ways which I had been taught were wrong for me, I still liked them. Also, they continued to be friendly, honest, and caring towards me and others. It was quite a wobble in my faith journey when I realised people who didn't go to church, nominal Christians and agnostics could be decent, caring human beings! I was surprised Christians didn't have the monopoly on ethical behaviour. I'd been given that impression by my church. It all sounds so arrogant now."

"What about your attitude towards the LGBTQI community? That must have done a 180 since you were a good Baptist girl!" Charity's eyes twinkle at me.

"Ironically, considering the present church debate, that happened when I was studying for the ministry. At that time there were some gay ministry students. This was before any official bans against gay ministers and elders. I just liked them as a group. There was Murray and Amy and Yvette. They were fun, creative, interesting people. Not stuffy, like other ministry students who were straight and conservative."

"Perhaps the pivotal moment was being invited to a 25th anniversary for a gay couple celebrating their relationship. Ian and Martin were a gregarious couple of guys. They were keen members of a church where they worked extremely hard to support that small church community which was working on being inclusive before that was fashionable. I'm talking the late 1980s here."

"That means," says Charity, counting on her fingers, "Ian and Martin must have been together before homosexuality was legal in New Zealand. The Homosexual Law Reform Act wasn't brought in until 1986."

"That's right. Most of their relationship had been 'illegal' in the eyes of New Zealand law. There were neither civil unions nor same sex marriage available at that point in New Zealand, so they weren't married then and never were. But they knew their first significant meeting was 25 years earlier, so they threw a party to celebrate. That changed my idea that gay people were 'Other' or different. From the perspective of the everyday functions of being married, these two were like any married hetero couple who'd been together for 25 years."

"That might seem reductive and patronising now but remember all I had to compare their relationship with were people like my parents and other hetero couples. I was looking at them and seeing much the same dynamics in many ways and wondering why the church was getting so excited about these so-called 'bad' relationships. Ian and Martin were loving and hospitable and creative. I didn't see anything wrong here!"

"From the outside, they weren't too different from my own parents. Perhaps a little more creative – they ran a coffee shop for years. Ironically, it was a coffee shop that my mother loved to visit. She may not have dreamed they were gay. One of them was a talented interior designer. They would bicker and argue and disagree with each other, but they were faithful, loving, and loyal, just like my straight Mum and Dad, though their history was more fraught."

Charity nods. "It's easier to reject people if you can think of them as different from you. You can easily reject those you don't mix with and never get to know well. It's how wars happen, isn't it? Soldiers on each side 'have' to think of their opponents as a-human or non-human objects to be able to kill them. Like that film based on fraternisation across the front line in WWI.[10] The troops were reassigned later because they'd got to know their enemies too well. They no longer felt OK about shelling the other side or invading their trenches."

I nod, remembering the movie *Joyeaux Noel* which had made a big impression on me at the time. "Yes, I remember it."

After a hesitation, I continue.

"You've heard me talk about dualisms. As women and/or lesbians, we find ourselves on one side of the gap between those lists. It's hard for the other side to reach across the gap to get to know the people who are Other to them."

I reach for a napkin and do my usual scrabble in my bag for a pen (why do I never put my pens away in the same pocket?) as I continue to talk, eventually scribbling down two short lists of words:

Unhelpful dualist thinking which divides us all into groups

GOOD	BAD
Male	Female
Straight	Gay
White	Black
Moral	Immoral
Trustworthy	Untrustworthy

"These are the relevant words for this conversation. We keep perpetuating these oppositions in western society. It takes a major event to get people together across this divide. Then the 'aha' moment happens, like those that happened to me. It becomes impossible to treat the Other as Other anymore because they've become human to us, become just like us. I remember thinking at that time that gay ministry students facing rejection by the Church were students just like me."

"We are!" replies Charity with a wobbly smile. Welling tears turn her eyes into teal-green pools. "Another iced coffee to celebrate, I think," she says and moves towards the counter.

"Make mine an iced chocolate," I ask.

When she returns, I've sketched a graph on the back of the napkin.

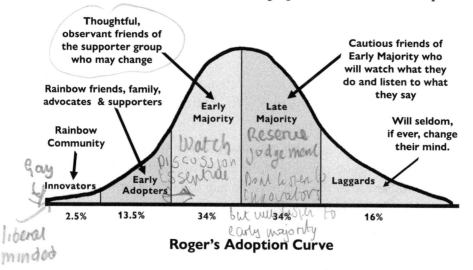

Roger's Adoption Curve

I notice she's dried her tears, though she still looks a bit fragile. I think some brain work might help to move our focus from the emotional to the cognitive for a while. Not that emotionality was wrong, but we can seldom get the logical part of our brain to work if we are in its archaic, generally emotional, sector. Charity looks curiously at my hastily drawn graph.

"Have you seen the Roger's Adoption Curve? It's another way of looking at 'ingroup' activity," I ask.

"A bell curve, seen those before," replies Charity.

"Yes, that's the shape. This one is about how readily people take up or adopt new ideas. We could draw lots of graphs for different ideas and you might be at a slightly different place on each one. Today, let's let this curve represent how church people adopt the idea of same-sex-attracted people being accepted for ordination as ministers or elders."

"Firstly, there are the Innovators, a ridiculously small percentage of the population. In this case they might be gay themselves, or liberally minded heterosexuals or people who have gay children or

32

siblings. Whatever, they know gays are not dangerous subversives! This might include a gay person who applied for the ministry. They know it could be dodgy. They are convinced however of their call and their right to be a minister in the Church if suitable in other ways. In other areas of life, these might be the inventors of a new product like the mobile phone."

Charity nods and I move my pen to the Early Adopters' section.

"The ministry students who were rainbow people in the first sector probably managed to get to training because they met some Early Adopters along the way. Maybe it was their family, their minister, or a lesbian lecturer at uni. Early Adopters see the new thing happening and like it. They are still a small percentage of the whole population. They know the new thing is unusual, but they like unusual. They like being first when a new thing is happening. In the world of mobile phones, Early Adopters will line up half the night to buy the new model at midnight when they go on sale."

Charity grins and proudly taps her new cell phone. Katy, her girlfriend, had lined up to buy it for her the previous week. Charity had been over the moon, not just about the cool features on the cell phone, but about what that act showed about how much Katy cared for her.

"Notice the percentages in these sections. Add them together and you get 16%. A new product does not reach mass market status if only this small number of the population have bought it. A company needs to influence the next group as well to get real entrée into the mass market." I move my pen to the Early Majority section of the graph.

"These Early Majority people aren't as keen on a new event, product, or idea as the previous two groups. But they watch the first two groups as they engage with the new product, or idea or behaviour. They keep an eye on how it's going. If there are few or no teething troubles, they will buy the product. This gets the product into mass market status. Marketers use this graph as a tool. Look at this example."

I pull the laptop toward me, click a few times, and show Charity an annotated Roger's curve in an online marketing article then sketch a simpler version on my napkin.

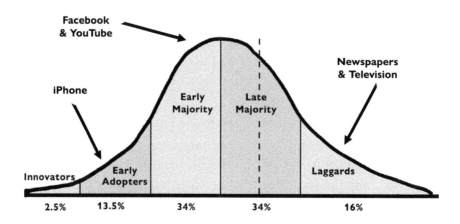

Marketing Version of the Roger's Adoption Curve

She pores over it as our iced coffee and chocolate arrive. I sip slowly as I watch her absorbed face and add some comments.

"This graph shows producers where to best advertise. See here at the top, the most popular platforms are Facebook and YouTube, for example. The bulk of the population use those. To advertise effectively, manufacturers should use those media platforms to influence the mass market."

"This marketing writer comments about the Early and Late Majority sections of the population. Look, he writes: 'This group relies heavily on the concept of social proof and wants proven process from credible source [sic] that demonstrates significant cost savings over the existing way of doing things.'"[11]

I add, "in the church, this group are those who reserve judgment on gay ministers or elders. That is, they hesitate until their Early Adopter friends experience gays in ministry and report that the sky didn't fall in. Or perhaps they experience a lesbian ministry leader. Or they might move to a church where gay elders have been common for a while. Their church might call a minister who has a same-sex partner. They might read a book by a rainbow Christian whose other work they have respected for a while. Like me, they might meet 'real, live gays.'"

I smile and wink to show Charity I know that's a patronising way of putting it. An idea occurs to me, and I continue.

"I remember the first funeral I ever took in the early 1990s. I was new to the parish and didn't know anyone. At the end of the service, I was standing by the hearse feeling a bit like a fifth wheel. A man I didn't know came up to me and said in a conversational, slightly wondering tone, 'My grandmother's funeral was taken by a woman minister.' It seemed a bit random. At first, I felt a bit of a freak. Later, I thought about it and decided he was adding up all the OK experiences he'd had with women ministers, (all two of them so far). He was slowly deciding we might be OK. On the question of women ministers, he would be an Early Majority man. It's the same process which can work for ministers and elders too if they happen to be in same sex relationships."

"That makes sense," responds Charity, "even if it must have been a slightly weird experience for you at the time."

"It was. As I said, I felt a bit of a freak until I worked it out later."

"It was a good example of the Early and Late Majorities needing what this writer calls 'social proof.' The two majorities shown here are different from each other. The Early Majority can talk with, listen to, and observe Early Adopters. They watch this group for clues as to how the change might go. Conversation between those two groups is vital."

"The Late Majority do not listen much to the Innovators and Early Adopters, but they will listen to the Early Majority," I add, then continue with another thought.

"This writer talks about 16% as the tip over into the mass market, but in the church the task is different. In our church, a rule has been established that a two thirds majority is needed for important legislation to be passed. So, the 'tipping point' for a vote to go through is past halfway. Half of the Late Majority needs to be on board to get the vote through."

My pen was following my words and now I put a mark just at the midpoint of the graph. It just about cut the Late Majority section in half.

Charity puts her finger on the marketing graph on my laptop at about the same place.

"Looks like Facebook and YouTube might be useful in that conversation!"

"Perhaps so," I reply. "Interestingly, those two platforms still aren't used very much by the traditional churches for communication, though the covid pandemic's changed that a little."[12]

"That voting rule still leaves about a third of the church unconvinced," comments Charity.

"Yes, it does, but it gets the exclusionary rule abolished. You need to know that, in most adoption curves, the 'laggards,' the last group, may never get on board with the relevant issue. They may also be implacably opposed to women ministers, newer versions of the Lord's Prayer, cell phones, maybe even a spherical planet or even sometimes electricity! (Just joking!) People vary on different issues, however. I am sure, though you are a progressive young woman, we'd find some habit or product or custom you refuse to adopt?"

Charity thinks for a while and then holds up her iced coffee glass. "Probably, but it wouldn't be coffee!"

She muses further. "I can see people tend to group with others with the same opinions on different issues. Like all the pro-war people tend to group together. They meet at the RSA or turn out on Anzac Day. I would be in the laggard group if this was a pro-war curve. I'd be proud to be there!" she finishes with a flushed face and a hint of surprise. "Where you come on the curve really does depend on what theme the curve is drawn for!"

"That's right. This means people in the Late Majority or Laggard groups on gay issues, might support other things in the church you also agree with. You both can be keen on community facing mission, or an innovative rebuild of a church after an earthquake or a foodbank on church grounds. It's not good for conservatives to judge gay Christians only on their sexual orientation. It's also not wise to judge a conservative only on their attitudes to the ordination of gay Christians."

"It's always good not to judge people on single issues.…. It's always good not to judge people!" adds Charity.

Nodding, I reply "This graph also shows, however, that it's easier to stay within the group with whom you are most comfortable. It also shows a person can be encouraged to increase the size of their group initially by agreeing with people almost like them or only a little bit different." I point to the line between the Early and Late Majorities.

"Like an Early Majority person might include an Early Adopter, or a Late Majority person might include an Early Majority person in their ingroup on an issue?" clarifies Charity.

"You've got it. A good example of this is the change in Professor David Gushee's circumstances. He is a professor of ethics, a convinced Baptist who taught against homosexuality in his university ethics classes. Recently, his sister came out to his family."

"Good on her!" Charity exclaims. "That must have been tricky!"

"In response, Gushee did a lot of research and changed his mind. He publicly apologised to students he might have hurt when he'd taught against homosexuality earlier. His announcement of his change of mind earned him a lot of flak from the fundamentalist/evangelical community in the States."

"I bet it did."

"I noticed after his book *Changing our Mind*, he published two more: *Still Christian: Following Jesus Out of American Evangelicalism*[13] and *After Evangelicalism: The Path to a New Christianity*.[14] The titles alone of the books suggest where he felt he had to go once his mind changed on the gay issue. Brian McLaren, who is a big name in the post-evangelical scene in America is a supporter of his journey.[15]

"I guess that's another problem. Once you change your mind on one issue, other related issues will also fall over. It's all interconnected," comments Charity.

"Mmm. Some are not prepared for the journey to be open ended and to trust it will take them to a good place. They may think it would be easier, safer and more comfortable to remain in the group they know and trust."

"Hmph!" retorts Charity. "Maybe safer, maybe easier, maybe more comfortable. It depends how long you can keep yourself insulated from the pain suffered by those you're excluding. What if your gay son or daughter has been too afraid to tell you who they really are? What if they become estranged from you, or worse? Then life's not more comfortable or easier. It has become definitely less safe!"

"Absolutely," I reply.

We both sit staring into our empty coffee cups and contemplate vacant seats we know of at family dinner tables with which we are familiar.

"So…" says Charity blowing her nose and wiping her eyes after a moment of quiet. "What might work using ingroup loyalty as an argument? First, it looks like only parts of some groups will successfully talk with parts of other groups?"

I nod in agreement. Clearing my throat, I speak past the lump in it.

"One strong argument is that there are many rainbow young people I've talked with who are devoutly evangelical. They want a bible-believing church. They want to do the right thing evangelically. They want to continue the worship they're used to. Yet, to gain acceptance, they must go to churches where they're not necessarily happy with the parish's theology."

"A gay friend once told me that acceptance was higher priority for him than theology. In the same conversation, however, he said he played worship songs as he drove to work. As he did, tears poured down because he missed Baptist worship so much. Conservative churches are missing a whole mission field. There are hurting gays and lesbians who would love to be welcomed into conservative churches, as long as it was unconditionally."

After a sip of coffee, I continue. "Another conversation I'd like to see happening in churches is around standards of sexual behaviour. You said it when we first met. It seems conservatives have this blanket idea all rainbow people are promiscuous (and by implication heterosexual young people aren't!). If conservatives knew the accepted rule was that both gay and straight ministers and elders should not act promiscuously, would that help?"

It was Charity nodding now. "I was shocked when I talked with a young conservative minister at the conference. I was saying it should be expected that ministers or elders, if they were in a relationship, would either have a civil union or a same sex marriage if they were rainbow community. He was surprised and said, 'So it wouldn't be anything goes?' How immoral does he think we gay Christians are, for goodness sake?"

I smile wryly. "That's a side effect of ingroups, conservative or liberal. They only 'hear' information damaging to the Other. They don't venture out far enough to check the facts. All homosexual people and all heterosexual people are, in fact, diverse groups. In both groups some are promiscuous, some are naturally celibate and seemingly asexual. Others have regular relationships which are sometimes great, sometimes good, and sometimes rocky. We are all human to the same extent."

"Think about it. What would happen if the rainbow community was more accepted in the church and same sex marriage was allowed and approved of by the church."

"Surely, that would help those couples to form more stable and longer term relationships, when they no longer live in a world where Christians are hostile to them?" I continue, "Maybe an 'ingroup' theme is that of responsibility in relationships. We could talk some more about that in relation to the Bible."

Charity nods. "That would be great. This has been so interesting. Can we meet same time, same place next week?" She jams the rainbow-sequinned beret on her head.

She looks and sounds better than the young woman who had come in, red-eyed, last week. Finding a framework to analyse what is going on always helps me. It has also helped her to think more clearly and carefully about this complex topic.

"Absolutely. Go well." I smile and wave as she leaves *The Cup*.

4 – The truth may be pure but it's never simple

[**CW**// Difficult church decisions: p. 41-42.]

Charity and I settle in with our coffees a week later. This week she's bohemian, with large gypsy earrings, red hair bundled up in a brightly coloured scarf wound round it like a turban, and jingling bracelets on tanned arms. I feel positively boring in my classic black working pants and top. Our coffees reflect our differences too. She's having a turmeric latte today, to my regular flat white.

Charity reports she's well into Haidt's book and finding it gripping. "It explains so much about how we come to our moral positions. Explained a lot about growing up with Mum and Dad too!" she grins. I'm pleased to see her looking more on balance.

"I've been wondering, what is the root meaning of 'sanctify'?" asks Charity. "As a concept it's always scared me a little. To sanctify seems a very, very holy, and important thing to do. To be sanctified sounds very serious." She waves her fore fingers on two hands in the air to indicate speech marks around 'very serious.'

"Well, it is!" I smile reassuringly.

"Using the word sanctified, very specifically for a specific purpose, is one way in which the seriousness of sanctification is honoured. The dictionary definition shows how many bases it covers for people who take it seriously." I turn my tablet round after finding the page.

"There's the first definition: 'set apart as or declare holy; consecrate.' Look at the synonyms they list – they are all very serious words, especially in this commitment phobic world of ours: 'consecrate, make holy, make sacred, bless, hallow, set apart, dedicate to God, anoint, ordain, canonize, beatify.'[16] You can see when something is sanctified it goes to the top of the pile religiously or spiritually."

Charity nods as her eyes dart over the list of words, so I continue.

"Those who believe in the power of sanctification, don't mess around with anything which has been sanctified. For instance, that's the basis of the respect usually paid to clergy – they've been ordained or sanctified. In Anglican and Catholic churches leftover communion elements are treated very carefully because in their eyes they are consecrated by the prayers said over them. Respect for something which is consecrated is becoming a foreign concept in our more egalitarian, less formal world."

"See here," breaks in Charity, pointing to the screen. "It's also about legitimacy. This dictionary says that another meaning of sanctify is to 'Make legitimate or binding by a religious ceremony.' And look at the example they've given: 'their love is sanctified by the sacrament of marriage.'"

"That brings us to one nub of how the debate about the place of gay people in the church has gone since the advent of same sex marriage. Gay marriage cuts across a deeply held conservative belief in the sanctity of marriage. Marriage isn't a sacrament in reformed denominations like ours. In the Catholic and Anglican world, it is. Reformed Christians, however, still feel that if marriage vows are made in the church, or in the presence of God, then they're binding. They see the relationship as sanctified or consecrated to God."

I point to the screen again. "See the synonyms listed here for this shade of the meaning of sanctify: 'approve, sanction, give the stamp of approval to, underwrite, condone, justify, vindicate, endorse, support, back, ratify, confirm, warrant, permit, allow, accredit, authorize, legitimize.'"

"Hmmm," murmurs Charity. "Those are all validation words, kind of… allowing words. You are really 'in' if you are sanctified through a recognised ceremony. Look, you're condoned…, permitted…, backed…, vindicated…. No wonder conservatives don't want to give this away easily. To 'allow' gays is to legitimize them."

"Yes, and here's the kicker. This third meaning is why it is so difficult for straight conservatives to let LGBTQI people 'in.' The third shade of meaning given for sanctify in this dictionary is 'free from sin; purify.'"

"What are the synonyms for that?" asks Charity more subdued now, but still curious. I scroll down the page to find the list given in the dictionary.

"Here they are: 'Purify, cleanse, free from sin, absolve, unburden, redeem, exculpate, wash someone's sins away, lustrate.'"

"What does 'lustrate' mean?" asks Charity, surprised at the word.

I do a quick cross check.[17] It's not a word I know well either.

"To 'purify by expiatory sacrifice, ceremonial washing, or some other ritual action.' For example, 'a soul lustrated in the baptismal waters.' It's not a word used much these days. It's from a Latin root. All the synonyms for this shade of the meaning of sanctify are about getting rid of sin so you become pure. That's what connects purity with sanctity."

"So…" murmurs Charity. "For conservatives, gays don't get to be connected with anything sanctified or pure (like being ordained) because conservatives believe the whole same sex relationship to be sinful."

She sits very still after she had spoken. Somehow, she looks smaller than when she had first come in. She heaves a heavy sigh.

"Why do I get the feeling we will never get there?" she asks and reaches for a tissue to stem the tears welling up. "It's like a circular argument. You're sinful so you can't be sanctified and because you can never be sanctified you can never 'sully' marriage with your 'sinful' relationship. And … only properly sanctified married people can be in the ingroup." She puts a hand over her heart and intones. "We will only be loyal to pure, sanctified, straight people."

"It is certainly an example of ingroup thinking," I agree.

I sigh heavily but carry on speaking. "These definitions explain why the religious authorities of the day were shocked by Jesus' behaviour. He seemed to seek out those we could call 'unsanctified' people. They were described as unclean or non-kosher in the Jewish faith of the first century. They were people with blemishes or illnesses, menstruating women, people who worked with any kind of animal products like leather, people who didn't keep the many little laws which had been developed to describe pure Jewish living."

Charity nods. "It would take time and money to do everything right and ordinary people simply couldn't always afford to be kosher."

"That was true then and is also true today. Being always on the right side of society and laws and religions often requires a higher socio-economic status." I continue, "remember Jesus being taken to the temple as a baby? That passage points out carefully that Mary and Joseph took birds for the sacrifice – only poor people took birds.

The gold standard was a lamb. By the way, that event's an example of a lustral ritual. The timing was largely because of Mary needing to be ritually 'cleansed' after the blood spilled in childhood. That simple little story is a good example of the purity and sanctity rules in Judaism affecting family life. Perhaps it was included to show Jesus in a good light to kosher former-Jews, who'd joined the budding Christian community."

I add, "most regular people in Jesus' world were 'unsanctified' or unclean. Only a few people living quite separated lives could really be completely kosher. As a rabbi, Jesus would have been expected to keep 'better company'. He's described as consorting with sinners, but they were probably simply ordinary people following a regular, but non-kosher life."

"That's right, he didn't only mix with the 'pure' people!" Charity sits up straighter. "He didn't! He talked to women, (unheard of at the time). He got around with ordinary men – and women – as his disciples."

"Yes, Mary Magdalene's a good example. She has the distinction of being named along with only a few other women followers of Jesus in the Second Testament.[18] That shows she was an important leader in the early Jesus movement groups."

Charity nods and sweeps on. "He touched lepers and other sick people. He deliberately touched a menstruating woman. He talked with foreigners too. Didn't expect them to have gone through the Jewish 'lustrous rituals!' If he were here today, he'd have been drinking coffee with us right now, wouldn't he?"

"Are you sure he isn't anyway?" I ask. We fall silent, feeling impossibly unsanctified but loved and accompanied. "I'm sure Jesus would frequent coffee shops today. I wrote a poem about it once." I flick through the laptop and find it.

"Have a read while I go and order us another cup of coffee. I think we've earned it. Another chai or something different?"

Charity points to the title of the poem, "I'll have a regular cappuccino with chocolate on top, thanks!"

Cappuccino Christ
Liturgy for a Coffeeshop

You kept the good wine till last, Jesus
and we read elsewhere
that you ate and drank
with all sorts of people.
Was it in their homes,
or in the taverns of your day?

If you had lived now,
would you have gone to coffeeshops together?
Ordering flat whites and long blacks
and double shot lattes perhaps?
Or are you a cappuccino man, yourself,
with chocolate or cinnamon on top?

What conversations
might I have had with you over the coffee cups
if you were here today!

We could have set the world to rights together,
saved the world ten times over,
sorting out all the big issues
like rights and responsibilities
and women's place,
our spoons fiddling with the froth on our cups
swirling the bowl, so all the foam is ours,
not left to some busy dishwasher out the back.

But I do talk in coffeeshops
and over cups of tea
(or perhaps a herbal infusion)

And I talk with the Christ,
only she is my friend
maybe my sister
or my colleague from work.

We put the world to rights,
save it a few times
debate our responsibilities
just the way you might have done
over a beaker or two of rough Israeli wine
two thousand years ago
with your men and women friends.

And we do not miss you now
because you are here
Cappuccino Christ
here in each of us
here in our gathering together

Cappuccino Christ
you are no transient foam atop a cup of coffee.
You are always there,
even when life
seems only dregs left in a cup when the party
is over.

You challenge
with the full strength of your stimulating love.
When the caffeine fails,
when the burst of friendship and camaraderie has gone
and the table is bare you are still there
keeping the best till last.
You comfort with milo and slippers at the end of the day
with calm and quiet promised in your word.

Wean us both from mother's milk
and from our sophisticated caffeine dependence
so we can see the signs of you in the world
and be signs of you to the world about us.

Susan Jones

"That's lovely," says Charity as I came back to the booth. "Could you email that to me? Is it published anywhere?"

"No, it's in a collection I've gathered, but I've never got 'out there.'"

"You should, it's helpful."

Our second coffees arrive, cappuccinos for both of us this time (I knew the title of the poem well). We sip reflectively, taking a break from both brainwork and heartache. We chat of this and that. How Charity's academic work is going, her father's recent stent operation and her mother's foray into local government as a city councillor. Then just as I sense we are almost winding up, Charity returns to the topic.

"I'm wondering if one way which might help the church in future could be based on the real value of purity or sanctity?" She pauses, biting her lip, as she often does when thinking hard.

"What say the church reassured all its members, that gay elders and ministers would be expected to follow the same expectations for their personal relationships as hetero elders and ministers? That would disappoint both homosexual and heterosexual young people who weren't married yet in this 21st century environment. But it could introduce another level of conversation about relationships."

I smile. "That's an idea. Certainly, I've often wondered in the context of this debate what makes a relationship sanctified or pure? One way we've seen in those definitions is that marriage, for example, is undertaken in the eyes of God and seen as a consecrated vow. But that turns to custard if there's not 'pure' behaviour to follow. Not pure only in the sense of chaste or celibacy within marriage, but pure in the sense of a good quality relationship."

Charity's face lights up. "You're right! Surely the point of a relationship is more about its quality than its structure. There are several more important factors we should require in relationships alongside the ceremonial blessing. Good relationships involve faithfulness to each other. They require mutual respect. They should be nonviolent. We would hope the partners love each other. Relationships I think, should have longevity as their goal, even if these days that seems a hard ask."

"All that is more important than the mix of genders in the relationship," she adds. "A relationship's ongoing quality surely matters even more than whether or not the marriage or union is blessed in a church."

Thinking about Charity's idea, I ponder my answer. "You know one of the most 'sanctified' marriages we've seen in relatively recent times was between Prince Charles and Lady Diana Spencer. The ceremony was conducted before the whole world, solemnised in probably the most important Abbey church in England. The Archbishop of Canterbury, the top churchman of the Church of England, officiated. The groom's mother is officially Defender of the Faith in the Anglican church. Yet that marriage was plagued by distrust. Right from the beginning there was unfaithfulness. So much so, the marriage ultimately ended in divorce. It may have been sanctified on paper and by protocol, but it wasn't a sanctified or 'pure' marriage in practice in the end. It was very sad for everyone involved, especially as it was all in the public eye. Yet there were no homosexual overtones to any of it."

"That's a powerful example of what goes on in quite a few heterosexual marriages. It doesn't mean we should devalue marriage. It does mean we should be realistic about the work needed to live up to the responsibility of being joined as a couple before God. Neither homosexuals nor heterosexuals have the monopoly on that," replies Charity. "Given recent history, I doubt my gay friends outside the church would thank any Christian for telling them how to manage their relationships. That's especially so when the church has such a bad press over infidelity and even abuse within it!"

I nod, and after a moment add, "There's a stumbling block we haven't tackled yet. The reason straight conservatives will not admit gays to ordination or marriage is that they believe the homosexual act for men or women is sinful."

"According to…?" asks Charity.

"According to the authority of the Bible. The authority of scripture is a strongly held value by the whole evangelical/conservative ingroup," I reply

"And authority is one of the criteria Haidt says is important to conservatives. Looks like we've got more talking to do," grins Charity as she gathers her things. "Same time, same place next week?

"You're the authority!" I smile back as, earrings swinging, she makes her way out the door.

5 – Who says?

[**TW**// Sexual violence: pp. 50-52.]

Back in *The Cup* the following week, wearing a man's black felt trilby perched at a jaunty angle, Charity digs into her large carry-all. She dives between her laptop and lecture notes and, I notice, uneaten lunch, to triumphantly emerge waving a Bible.

"I thought we might need this today!" she grins. "It's a bit dusty because I read the Bible online these days when I'm catching up on blogs and podcasts. It's easier to stay with the one device."

"I find the same when I'm writing reflections. There are good search engines now to find the passages that come to mind when you're writing."

"Wouldn't internet metaphors would be good for spiritual concepts?" muses Charity as our coffees arrive. "The Bible is one massive inbox, with lots of e-mail messages from the divine. Impure thoughts should be sent to the trash, perhaps! Mm, must think more about that."

"Last time we'd got to thinking about how some Christians think gays should be trashed because they were not sanctified enough." It's time to get started.

"Yes, according to the conservative debaters at national conference, the Bible doesn't allow us to even contemplate that a gay relationship is OK in any shape or form," responds Charity. "What's with that? They seem to believe things about the Bible that I don't believe. For them the Bible is right up there with the Holy Spirit. Sometimes, I wonder if it is even more important than Jesus in their thinking."

"Interesting you should say that," I reply. "A writer I read recently argues we treat the Bible as an idol when we read the Bible literally. We idolise it when we expect the words on the page to have only their surface meanings. He talks about literalism killing the spirit when we try to pin it down to an unchanging form.[19] Consequently, he urges care in reading the Bible."

"You said David Gushee had looked at key passages people quote when using biblical authority in their arguments." Charity turns to accept the Americano with hot milk which she had ordered.

"I brought his *Changing our Mind* book with me today," I said. "In the introduction to the biblical passages, he describes five groups to whom he's writing."

"The first are believers who strongly believe in the authority of the scriptures for Christians. Secondly, those prepared to entertain a variety of ways of choosing, interpreting and making use of specific bible passages. Then those who feel biblical investigation is necessary background for moral decision making."

"The fourth group he's writing for are those who know that on top of biblical exegesis we need also consider context; when the Bible was written and today when it's being read and applied. His fifth group of intended readers are those who feel honesty and fair-mindedness, along with Holy Spirit's help, are important."

"He suggests then that those who might come to agree with him will need an open mind," deduces Charity.

"Yes. I think that applies to both liberal and conservative Christians. Somewhere I read his advice to liberals about what NOT to do when discussing LBGTQI issues with conservatives. It lists everything I've heard liberals argue on the floor of national conference![20]

"Ooh, must read that," says Charity. "Listening to the liberals at the conference, I've sometimes wondered how prepared they really were to hear other points of view. What does Gushee say about the key passages? Which ones does he zero in on?"

"Let me see," I reply, reading through the book's contents. "In the First Testament he looks at two Genesis passages, one in Leviticus, another in the book of Judges. The Second Testament passages he analyses are two Gospel ones: Matthew and Mark, then three from the letters to the Romans, the first letter to the Corinthians and to Timothy. There are others too which refer generally to sex or marriage."[21]

Charity opens her Bible at the first book, Genesis. "The first Genesis passage is just about the creation of humankind, isn't it?"

"Yes, people being created male and female, and the woman being created as a response to the man's loneliness," I respond.

Charity is quick to point out the ambiguity of my statement. "Except that as Phyllis Trible points out, the first creature is not a man but is an undifferentiated 'earth creature.' Gender only appears at the second creation of humanity where the man and the woman are created at the same time."[22]

"You're right, of course. I should have been more precise in what I said. Trible argues the Hebrew word we translate 'Adam' supports that. Though, of course, it's significant for our context that the story still ends up with a different-sex couple. It's the narrator who connects this to marriage."

"What about the other Genesis passage? Chapter 19?"

Again, I consult the book. "The Genesis and Judges stories are similar narratives. Both should have trigger and content warnings for sexual violence. Are you OK with me going on?"

Charity swallows and nods, taking a sip of coffee, to fortify her. "I think so," she says. I continue watching her carefully.

"In both, men from the community want to sexually assault males who are guests in local homes. They are similar stories, but with different results, neither of them good for women. In the Genesis story, Lot offers his daughters instead, an offer not accepted, fortunately. In Judges, the host offers his concubine. Unfortunately, this offer is accepted. She is tortured and raped until nearly dead. Then she is torn into pieces by her master."

"Eeew, not a Sunday school kind of story, then!" exclaims Charity. She breathes deeply. "Want some chocolate cake? We might need it to get through this."

She bolts from the table to get the food. Taking a break to compose herself, I think. This is very difficult stuff. When she returns, we savour the richness of the chocolate mud-cake with cream on the side. Comfort eating has its place!

"No use getting yoghurt if you're already eating chocolate cake like this," mumbles Charity through her second mouthful. I wait for her to signal when she wants to return to our discussion. It is a moment and a few spoons full later when she comments.

"I don't think I've heard this preached in church."

"No, not often preached about in churches, for obvious reasons, so it hasn't been well interpreted. You'll know that Phyllis Trible included that story in her book on *Texts of Terror*.[23] Her analysis makes sobering reading."

Charity skims chapter 19 of Genesis with one hand and continues eating cake with the other. "This Genesis 19 story revolves around the visit to Sodom of angels of God. They're there to investigate whether they can find any righteous people in Sodom. The city is known for its wickedness and vice... but if they can find righteous people ... the city might be saved according to the deal Abraham has made with God."[24]

"That's the one. This story's become culturally associated with a prohibition on homosexuality. The outrage of the story is greater than that, though. The sins of Sodom shown here include gang rape. That's something neither homosexuals nor heterosexual communities condone today, whoever the participants. It was also a major violation of the Eastern hospitality rule of the time that visitors to a town should be well-treated. Lot's willingness to sacrifice his daughters is unacceptable as well, yet not about homosexuality at all. The whole incident is made more horrendous and blasphemous because the original threat of sexual assault is made towards heavenly messengers. The most damning aspect of this story, however, is the underlying threat of violence."

"Look what Gushee writes," I add. "'The parallel story in Judges 20:5 makes absolutely clear that it was violence the men wanted, including sexual violence, and violence they inflicted.'"[25]

"Further on," I continue, "he tells us that this story of Sodom and Gomorrah is referred to later in the Bible in over 16 different passages. The twin cities are used as a symbol of ultimate depravity – you'll have heard them referred to even today. However, in the later biblical references, the depravity is not linked to homosexuality. He goes through the different descriptors. The sins of Sodom and Gomorrah are typified as adultery, lying, pride or too much ease, and carelessness and other sins. Even in the two passages which do talk of "unholy interest in 'other flesh,'" the reference is specifically to sexual interest in angels."[26]

"I can see why," says Charity quietly, "if conservatives thought this passage related to homosexuality, that it would frighten people enormously. This is horrendous stuff viewed from any sexual orientation or gender perspective. It certainly should come with trigger and content warnings!"

"Gushee likens it to the fear of gang rape in prison. Look at what he cites here from William Loader: "The men of Sodom want gang rape. They are more interested in men than in Lot's daughters because in a patriarchal society men held greater worth, and thus their violation was viewed as a greater offence than violating a woman.""[27]

Charity has turned a little pale, but is holding together, so I carry on, trying to get over this heavy ground as lightly and as quickly as I can.

"He also touches on something many people think underlies vilification of gay men by heterosexual society. It's about the point of the request to violate the angels. This was specifically to treat them as women might be treated during the sex act, especially a violent sex act. As Gushee writes here, 'in sexist social systems the most outrageous thing you can do to a man is to treat him like a woman.'[28] Many writers think gay men (and perhaps effeminate straight men too) are looked down on by straight men, because of this assumption."

"What assumption?" asks Charity.

"That one of the men in homosexual intercourse must be acting as the 'woman' in the partnership and is therefore demeaning his masculinity. When you analyse the number of epithets used for gay men, they mostly suggest a feminine or effeminate character – poufter, pansy, etc. – which bears out what Gushee and others are saying."

"That's depressing for a woman to hear!" exclaims Charity. "You mean prejudice against gay men, homophobia, comes out of a basic misogyny?"

"That's one of the threads of the arguments which underlie this debate," I agree, glad that her appropriate anger is helping her to tolerate this difficult story. "A lot of this is quite unconscious for most people, male and female, of course."

"Wow." She sits for a minute, absorbing the enormity of this discovery, then asks, "how does Gushee conclude his chapter on these passages?"

"Strongly. Look here, he writes that these two chapters '...are narratives with huge implications for the ethics of war, prison, gender, violence and rape. But they have nothing to do with the morality of loving covenantal same-sex relationships'"[29]

"Thank God," breathes Charity. The two words are a sincere prayer. She looks as if she had been through a battle herself. Others who point the finger at the LGBTQI community have little idea how personal this is. Actual human beings, as Charity and her community are, find this inherent rejection of them as a person extremely hurtful.

My thoughts are racing. This might be a political battle within the church, but it is personal to many people. Charity's reaction to the implication of misogyny as a driver of the more aggressive side of homophobia shows this. Not only gay women feel rejected by homophobia, straight women do also. Homophobia is based on an underlying phobia against the Feminine in general, whether straight or gay.

Conservative, anti-gay, straight men and women may feel good about rejecting what they label as sinful and getting it out of their sight. But real, live people with real, live families are living the reality they are rejecting. It's hard to realise a large part of the church had for years associated gang rape and sexual violence with your minority sexual orientation. Or, that your church, at best, hadn't thought about these passages very much. It's gut wrenching too, to absorb that this passage had always sat within Holy Scripture. It appears to condone Lot's offer to substitute young virginal girls as the object of sexual violence, since there is no warning against or condemnation of his offer to the angry men at his door. It wasn't only the gay community getting doctrinally battered here.

"I don't want to sound banal, but we probably need another cup of coffee," I say out loud.

"Yes," says Charity, wiping away her tears. "And let's talk of pretty kittens and sweet young lambs or something else impossibly cute and innocent! I think I'm only going to be able to cope with one set of passages at a time. We may be coming here for some weeks!"

"Fine by me," I reply. "This is important work, even if it is hard."

6 – What is the law and who should follow it?

[**TW**// Sexual violence, abuse & paedophilia; suicidal ideation: pp. 54, 55, 59-62.]

Charity and I meet again the next week.

Despite her bright emerald-green cap with gold trim, she's looking tired. She tells me it's the result of several significant deadlines for her courses the previous week.

"I'm on long blacks today. Pulled a couple of all-nighters," she smiles ruefully. "It'd be better if I learned to get started on essays sooner. Then maybe there wouldn't always be this last-minute rush. Hey, like your top – that flame colour suits you!"

"Thanks!" I reply. "We are a colourful pair today." Knowing I was meeting Charity that morning I had thought I should be brave and take a break from my habitual black theme. Seeing the emerald cap, I was glad I had. "So, with assignments and all, you won't have had much time to think about horrible Bible passages."

"I have! Yesterday after I got my Psych 203 paper in, I looked up Leviticus and had a read through. My goodness, what a lot of commandments, about all sorts of things! And what a draconian set of punishments. People were lucky to stay alive in those times if the religious authorities ever followed up on the rules as written. Perhaps the rules were just there to frighten people and were seldom enforced?"

"I don't know," I reply. "There's everything from food laws, to relationship rules, to idol worship, to naughty children. Even drinking when going to the tabernacle merited the death penalty in that world."

"What do scholars say about the passages quoted in the gay debates?" asks Charity. "Where are they again? Two in Leviticus, but different chapters."[30] She finds the place. "Looks like gay behaviour is detestable according to this piece here."

"Well, behaviour of male gay persons anyway," I reply. "The same principle applies as we discussed last week. Male on male relationships were particularly disliked because they were believed to render at least one of the males passively penetrated. You found the word 'detestable' in the New International Version of the Bible, but the Old King James Version called it an 'abomination.'"[31]

"David Gushee uses that word when he explains it like this. 'The penetrated recipient allows himself to be treated like a woman, which is itself seen as an abomination. The abomination is because of its profound violation of hierarchical male-dominant gender roles.'"[32]

"But..." Charity is obviously not believing what she is hearing.

"He points out that 'if this is the reason for the ban, it raises questions for any Christian who does not share beliefs in the lesser worth and dignity of women,'"[33] I add.

"Exactly!" Charity can't contain herself; I can tell by the green flash in her eyes. "You know the worst effect on me of last week's discussion was that underlying misogyny? Surely, we don't need to perpetuate that anymore. Can't we all grow up!?" She is really annoyed, and I can sense, quite deeply hurt under her indignation.

I think carefully before I speak.

"It's a really deep gut issue for us in Western society," I respond. "I find it in the passive resistance I get even from women when I suggest God be referred to in the feminine gender sometimes. You can tell that for them, thinking of God as feminine is no promotion for the status of the divine. Rather, they see it as a demotion which makes some men and some women very uneasy."

Charity breaks in. "Have you noticed with some older people what happens when you talk for a long time praising or promoting women? They begin to get fidgety as if men are being given a hard time. As if to praise or promote a woman is bad mouthing men at the same time."

I nod. "For Christians, it's an influence from an ancient philosophy of dualistic thinking. We talked about this a few weeks ago. It crops up all the time underneath conversations I have on gender and orientation issues." I dig around in my bag for my pen which is as elusive as usual and, reaching for a napkin, draw a vertical line. On each side of the line, I write words in pairs.

"Remember? The key pairing is bad and good, that sets the whole scene for the relative valuing of all the other pairs of words. The problem is that we set a kind of abyss between the two words in each oppositional pair, and we set them in opposition, forgetting that in most cases there is a continuum between the two concepts. These are the pairs relevant to this argument. Remember some of these? Look."

Qualities Treated as Dualisms

BAD	GOOD
Female	Male
Passive	Active
Gay	Straight
Private	Public
Body	Mind
Extramarital Sex	Marital sex

"These come from dualistic Persian philosophy which influenced Zoroastrianism, which in turn influenced Jewish exiles in Babylon as far back as 586 BCE. Obviously, Christianity is in turn heavily influenced by Judaic ideas. Dualism simply points out types of matter or concepts which cannot be reduced to each other. But the version Christianity struggles with here, is ethical dualism."

"Ethical dualism?" asks Charity.

"In ethical dualism, moral value is given to each part of the pairing of words/concepts. One side is considered 'good' and the other considered 'bad'."

"That means these dualisms have survived down deep in the western human psyche for centuries, millennia even!" Reluctantly, Charity is obviously impressed.

"Yes, that's the western worldview. In Eastern societies an ethical view of the human person is more nuanced. They follow more a Ying-Yang philosophy. The idea is we are a mixture of these 'good' and 'bad' characteristics. The end-goal is to integrate them rather than oppose them in our lives." I sketch a Ying/Yang symbol on the napkin alongside the dualisms.

"You can see this symbol's telling us we contain both light and shadow. It illustrates there is also darkness in our lightness and lightness in our darkness. This philosophy originated from China. It teaches that forces which seem opposite, or contrary, can complement each other and be interconnected and interdependent. They might even give rise to each other as they interrelate."

I think for a minute.

"I guess a similar symbolic representation of the dualistic approach would be this." I draw a box, half of which was black and half white, with a clearly delineated line down the middle of it.

"The 'pure Christian' position is the white half of the box on the left?" asks Charity, looking at the two diagrams intently, absent-mindedly pushing her cap half off her head.

"Yes. The difficulty many Christians get into is when they try to deny there is even any dark side to us at all. That's when repressed desires and emotions can become dangerous."

"I remember trying to be all on the white and pure side when I was hiding being gay as a teenager. I realise now I'd been taught the dualistic way of looking at things and I 'knew' being gay was all bad," remembers Charity. "So, I got the impression it was important I stayed away from all types of 'badness' as defined by my church." She sighs, remembering the confusion and tension of those days.

I join her in a quiet sip of coffee. It was good to take a break.

After a while I divert back to Gushee.

"I get the impression that David Gushee in his chapter on Leviticus is pointing out that there are many 'abominations' listed here. Many of them we take no notice of at all now. You'll have seen that satirical piece about whether or not people should follow all the Levitical rules?"

"Yes," Charity grins. "I was binge watching *West Wing* the other night. The scriptwriters used some of that for President Bartlett to put down a conservative female radio host. She soon realised he was serious. I looked it up online. It was first published in 2000 in response to Dr Laura Schlessinger's conservative radio show in the US."[34]

"I love that piece," she continues. "It includes questions about Levitical passages including selling your daughter into slavery, and whether you can play American football without touching pigskin. It even has neighbours objecting to animal sacrifices and a whole lot more, which are not commandments we would try to obey. Now, I find it funny. I wonder what a conservative would think of it. I'll have to ask one of my friends about that."

I point with my pen to the mind-body line on the two lists of words on the napkin.

"The dualism lists help to explain why sexual sins seem to get a lot of attention. It's from this mind-body pairing. Anything to do with the body is rated negative. This includes sex, both straight and gay, it includes menstruation and emotional outbursts."

Charity nods. "Anything in the 'forbidden', repressed part of a life tends to take on a dark kind of fascination for people. We learned about repression in Psych 201."

Unconsciously she takes on a teaching tone in her voice.

"Repressed emotions are feelings we bury without realising it. For instance, we might grow up in homes or churches where anything to do with the body is treated as a matter for shame. We learn to hide away any thoughts or feelings we have associated with that. The problem is the rigid, narrow environment. We don't get a chance to work through those emotions before they are pushed down out of sight. So, lurking inside, unknown to us consciously, are raw unprocessed emotions. The problem comes when something triggers them into being expressed to others. Because we are unused to expressing negative emotions, when we are forced into doing it, it's often an explosive and uncomfortable experience for everyone."

I nod, grinning back at her. "Well said, Prof! It's the negative emotions which are effectively banned from being expressed in environments where being 'pure' and 'good' is valued over being real with all your emotions, negative and positive."

Charity agrees. "I wonder if some conservatives adamantly against expressions of gay love could have had bad experiences in younger life. Especially now, we're hearing of abuse in boarding schools and care homes, which would have been traumatic."

"I think that is probably true," I agree. "It would account for the great swell of raw, unprocessed negative emotion towards homosexuality in national church conference debates. Sometimes it would have traumatically hurt and shamed the person as a younger child or adolescent, the kind of age when such trauma bites deep."

I think for a moment and pick my next words carefully.

"Equally, perhaps, they found they experienced some desire during abuse, or game-playing or experimentation. They might be extra-ashamed later. That could well have been repressed or suppressed (where you know what you're pushing down). Their sense of shame could easily be triggered during public debates and discussions in the church. That would generate disgust with the whole subject as well as self-disgust. Some may not even now know consciously what makes them feel that way. Shame is an exceedingly difficult emotion to process in a judgmental atmosphere."

"I suppose," comments Charity, "those who are anti-gay may not know of the distinct possibility of being bisexual. It's common knowledge in the rainbow community that people can be attracted by both men and women. If you're a black and white thinker, that would seem like you should be either gay or straight, nothing in-between. If such a male felt even a little desire towards a boy or man, he would assume he was gay. If he thought that was terrible, his feelings would be chaotic."

"I hadn't thought through that far," I reply. "I think that would be right. Of course, abuse is always wrong," I continue, "whether it is heterosexually administered or homosexual in its pairing. I don't know if Christian hetero men always realise that women fear abuse too. Women usually fear it from men. That is, the abuse for them is heterosexual and just as much a problem as male paedophiles preying on young boys, or adult males approaching other males."

Charity nods. "We learned in Psych that the paedophilic urge is not necessarily a homosexual one. I get mad when Christians just lump homosexuals and paedophiles together."

She continues slowly. "Both the dualisms list and that idea of prior harm could explain the highly charged atmosphere in the national church conference when this was discussed. It just seemed people were getting very, very uptight. This is simply a decision among many which needs careful thought and decision making. It doesn't necessarily require the level of emotional engagement I was sensing."

I agree with Charity. The debates I'd experienced certainly carried much greater emotional weight than the subject matter required.

"Negative emotions are not often dealt with in the context of the Christian narrative. Yet, it's there in many bible stories. The return of the so-called prodigal son. The shame Tamar felt when she saw that she had been passed over by her father-in-law Judah. The shame Ruth might well have felt gleaning for her daily food with other poor women. Peter's shame at denying Jesus. There are all sorts of shame about all sorts of things in the bible stories. I don't think I've ever heard them preached about."

"You've preached about them," says Charity. "I remember that series last year on dealing with negative emotions. I found it very helpful at the time."

"I meant I hadn't heard anyone preaching to me on it. It was more the case in my childhood church that the preaching I experienced as a listener generated negative emotions in me and then told me that was a sin!"

"That's a horrible cycle to get caught up in! How does David Gushee end his chapter on the Levitical passages?"

"He says that the passages are important ones, but that 'they do not resolve the LGBT issue.'"

Charity leans back in her seat and counts off on the fingers of one hand.

"A few things have come clear for me today. One is there are many, varied factors which create this debate in the church. Only part of it is how we interpret the Bible. The other is the context in which that interpretation takes place. People come to this issue with all sorts of emotions lurking in the unconscious part of their psyche. They have no idea they are there. Short of psychoanalysing everyone, I don't see how this can be shifted."

"Want to let this topic go then?" I ask.

"No. It's depressing and painful, but the more I know the better." Charity smiles at me tiredly. "But can we take a break? I've got midterms next week. What say we meet in three weeks from now? Same day and time and place?"

"Sure, "I said adjusting my phone calendar. Just before she rises from the table, I put my hand on her arm, so she looks at me.

"Just remember, Charity, Love surrounds you..."

"...every moment of every day." Smiling, she joins in with the familiar benediction which we use in church each Sunday and means so much to her

"Thanks."

I catch the glint of tears in emerald eyes as she turns to leave, her cap back at its cheeky angle.

This is hard stuff. The church community preaches everyone is loved by God and expounds the ubiquity of grace. That our part of the Church also selectively excludes a whole sector of society is very hard to process for someone like Charity who is part of that sector.

I remember a suicidal phone call I'd answered from the young woman now swinging out on to the pavement. Charity had not felt safe or comfortable during the period she was wrestling with coming out to the church. We'd reminisced about it just the other day. She had said she remembered the feeling well.

"It was really black," she'd said. "Looking back now it felt like I was in a black hole. I can see now there was some goodness and love and positive attention coming my way, but it just got sucked inside and down a kind of evil drain. It didn't seem to be able to do me any good at all. All I could see was hopelessness and dead ends. All that made any impression on me were the cruel words and rejection."

I remembered that time well too. "What made the difference? What was the light at the end of the tunnel for you?"

"Two things," she'd replied. "Funnily enough, one was that phrase of yours you use in church 'Love surrounds you every moment of every day.' That seemed to suggest that even my horrible black hole of a life was being held in Love. I think on its own that wouldn't have been enough, but it pierced the darkness sufficiently that I got the courage and energy to phone Lifeline. They really 'heard' me. From there I got some ideas about how to connect with other resources, like counselling and psychotherapy. I also did the practical thing of going to the doctor and getting antidepressants which helped break the mood cycle. Later, when I was more together, spiritual direction helped enormously too."

I'm glad she had finally seen that light. One of the horrible things for people trying to accompany someone who is contemplating suicide is that you sense only part, if anything, of what you are saying is getting through. Also, you can see that blackness blotting out the truth that there are people who care for them whose worlds would be made a lot worse if they left this life. I can't now imagine my experience or our church without Charity, for example. And, even when a young person is estranged from their parents, their suicide totally affects those parents for the rest of their lives.

I remembered being glad to hear Charity say last week, "Yes, I can see that now and celebrate it. But, when that horrible grey-black cotton wool of depression is wrapping round you, it can seem there's no one there."

"Horrible," I had replied. We had sat in a remembering silence, honouring the importance of that time in Charity's life.

How jumpy, angular and angry Charity'd been in her closet phase. Now she was out to her family and church, she is a radiant, well-adjusted student. She's doing well at her studies and is a natural leader in the younger adults group. Realising she is loved precisely as the gay person she knows herself to be is transforming her life. I am no longer concerned she will be another suicide statistic as I had been two years ago. She no longer sucks energy from all around her as she had in her previously depressed state. Now she adds energy to any gathering. She spreads bright light and warmth and love with her wherever she goes. What did it say about the kind of church we were in if they didn't want elders and ministers like her?

It was bad enough for Charity finding out the depth of the animosity towards homosexual relationships. I'm also finding it tough to encounter again the low opinion of women held over millennia. The interpretations we're working on underline widespread disdain within western society for the Feminine. They emphasise the general contempt held towards those who act in passive or receptive modes.

The corresponding valuing of force, penetration and strength overall within a patriarchal society is a little frightening too. I am a relatively 'successful' professional woman comfortably off. I am a privileged woman in my society. Yet I too feel the implicit devaluing of what I say and what I do and write. Do I and do other women have a place in this world? Is this how people in the gay community feel all the time when they encounter homophobia?

Shaking my head to rid it of these depressing reflections, I open my journal's front cover to the poem which I paste in the front of all my journals as I begin them. I need its message today.

In Stormy Moments

On days when the sea is flat calm,
sun shining from an azure sky,
it is OK to be me.

In stormy moments,
when a squall blows up, however,
it is a different story as my little boat
is tossed about by rejection, prejudice, and vitriol.

Then I shrink, smaller than I am,
unsure anymore if there is a place for me in this world,
whether or not
to simply slip over the side and be no more.

But, as I burrow down in my small boat,
I find, sleeping there, my Self,
that wise, mysterious me
who knows my worth,
who reminds me,
even as the wind screams overhead:

"You are… You are loveable…You are loved."[35]

7 – Lost in translation

[**CW**// Paedophilia: pp. 65-68.]

It is a month before I meet Charity again. She'd gone home after exams to take a break with her parents. It was an opportunity to clear her mind of study pressure before she began her second semester papers.

I wait in *The Cup* for her to arrive, wondering how she feels about resuming our focused biblical studies. I had good news she would enjoy as we looked at the two Second Testament passages in the letter to the Corinthian church and the first letter written to Timothy. Because they were written after the advent of Jesus, Second Testament references tend to carry more weight with Christians. Though, when they make their arguments, conservatives tend not to lighten up on the First Testament verses we'd already considered either.

Charity comes through the door. She's wearing a black beanie with rainbow stripes across the front. She gestures to the counter. I nod. Yes, I had placed my order. She joins the queue. It is quite short today. It'd been quieter in *The Cup* for the past fortnight. Students were still coming back from their mid-year break.

"How was your break?" I ask as she arrives at the table.

"Great! It was so good to be at Mum and Dad's and there was just enough snow to get a little skiing done even!" Charity did have some ski tan, I noticed, as she pulled off the beanie. The paler raccoon-like patch where her goggles had been made the whole effect a little bizarre. There had been an unseasonably early fall of snow and some ski-fields were open unofficially.

"Hey!" she adds, before I can comment. "I came across a fascinating article on biblical translating this week as I was messing around looking for some info on the Corinthian and Timothy clobber passages." Her eyes sparkle greenly.

"'Clobber' passages?"

"That's what the guy called them. I think it's a great name: The Six Clobber Passages."

"Hmm," I said. "Gushee thinks that's one of the disrespectful things liberals do, labelling them as clobber passages, leading conservatives to think that liberals are making a joke of it all."

"Oh," said Charity thoughtfully. "I'd never thought of it that way, but I guess that's true. Just as well I only said it to you. I'll not do that again. Interesting what can put people off someone from a different perspective."

"That's right. It's a touchy subject with a lot riding on it, so people get touchy around it. Well, don't keep me in suspense, spill it!" I say, leaning forward.

Charity gets out her tablet and begins tapping and scrolling.

"What got me started was Dad's comment last week that the word homosexual was a relatively modern word. He thought it dated back only as far as the 19th century. So...."

I smile. This was part of the good news I had brought to our meeting. Synchronicity was at work. "So... 'homosexual' can't have been the word used in the original context? Or in the earliest translations, anyway."

"Exactly!" said Charity. "This guy was researching just what we've been talking about. He collects European-language bible translations. Some dated back to just after the Reformation. He can't read the languages, so called on friends who know German, Swedish and Norwegian to read for him."[36]

"His friend read one of his German language bibles dating from the 1800s. They found in both Leviticus 18:22 and 20:13 it was **not** written, "Man shall not lie with a man..." but, "Man shall not lie with young boys as he does with a woman."

"So, they looked at the Corinthians and Timothy passages where there's a word...let me see.... *Arsenokoitai*...."

I gasp.

"What?"

"Never mind, carry on," I said

"That word is translated in that edition of the German Bible as 'boy molesters.' The German word used is...."

She scrolls further down the article.

"*Knabenschander* – *knaben* for boy and *schander* for molester."

So, what is being banned or sanctioned here is not relationships between two male consenting adults, but pederasty – sexual abuse of children."

I nod, but Charity doesn't notice and rushes on with her information.

"So, this researcher… Ed… asked his friend when this word began to be translated as homosexual. He looked at different German translations of the Bible. His conclusion was the word homosexual wasn't used in German translations before 1983."

"Wow, I didn't know it was that late," I said. "The word homosexual was created in the German language, wasn't it? In the previous century? I remember seeing an article about that."[37]

"Yep. Germans developed and used the word from the latter half of the 19th century," says Charity. "I wrote down this quote from a *New Yorker* article I found online. 'In 1869, an Austrian littérateur named Karl Maria Kertbeny, who was also opposed to sodomy laws, coined the term "homosexuality."'[38] They could have changed the translation any time they did a new Bible translation, but they didn't until the German NIV was printed in 1983."

"Why then?" I ask, thinking the 1980s was the decade when all the fuss began in the New Zealand Presbyterian churches. I wonder if the change in translation reflects the cultural context of the time.

"Well," says Charity meaningfully, looking me straight in the eye, "the German version of the NIV was funded by an American publishing company."

"Wow," I slump back on my seat. "Wow."

"In fact," says Charity, "This Ed doing the research checked a lexicon of the type which Martin Luther would have used for his translation in the 16th century. In that lexicon published in 1483, (the year Luther was born) the word comparisons go Greek: *arsenokoitai* to Latin: *paedico* and *praedico* which are then given as *pederasty* in English and *Knabenschander* in German. Martin Luther would have gone with that equivalence."

She continues, "the King James Version in England used, 'abusers of themselves with mankind,' for *arsenokoitai*. The first change from that was not until 1946 with the Revised Standard Version which translated *arsenokoitai* as homosexual."

"Why were they writing about pederasty? Was it a problem in the society of the first century?"

"Yes, it was. Listen to this." Charity scrolls further down the article and reads from her tablet.

> It turns out that the ancient world condoned and encouraged a system whereby young boys (8-12 years old) were coupled by older men. Ancient Greek documents show us how even parents utilized this abusive system to help their sons advance in society. So for most of history, most translations [sic] thought these verses were obviously referring the pederasty, not homosexuality![39]

She turns to me, cheeks flushed partly in anger and partly in relief.

"So all this gay bashing has been based on a mistranslation!"

"A bit like the word virgin when Mary's story is told," I reply. "The original wording is 'young woman.' The translation made it 'virgin' assuming an unmarried young woman in those times would have been a virgin."

"They are both pretty important mistranslations!" retorts Charity.

"Indeed, they are. David Gushee," I say, waving his book, "has much the same material about what original words were used. The timing of the change in translation is new to me, however. I thought you'd like his conclusion and information. Of course, what is being written against here, should be written against. The older men were usually married, so they were committing adultery against their wives. As well, they were indulging in a 'relationship' (if we can call it that) which was grossly unbalanced as to power dynamics. 8-12 years old is incredibly young. This is straight out paedophilia referred to here."

"As we were saying last time, people unfortunately sometimes mix homosexuality and paedophilia," replies Charity firmly. "A homosexual man or woman is not automatically a paedophile. We know heterosexuals can be paedophiles as well. The dynamics which cause paedophilia are unique to those perpetrators. We did the psychology of sexuality last year in Psych."

She goes on.

"I feel like taking out a full-page advertisement in the paper or on YouTube proclaiming this mistranslation. Say I applied for ministry and had a girlfriend. I'd expect to be required to be in a civil union or a marriage and be faithful to it. I know ministry needs to set high standards of morality. I'm not talking about abuse or preying on younger children. I wouldn't tolerate it if another lesbian or a gay man was doing that in the church. In the same way, I wouldn't tolerate abuse if it were a heterosexual perpetrator."

"The conversation needs to be elevated to a different level," she continues. "Not who is in this relationship or how they are doing it, but why. And the 'why' of relationships needs to be about the highest good of the other – love, mutuality, respect, non-violent treatment of each other, safety, companionship, spiritual friendship."

"I couldn't agree more," I reply, loving her passionate acuity. "Who's going to tell everyone about this? I don't think you are serious about the full-page ad?"

Charity grins cheekily. "No? Are you sure?"

She sobers up a little.

"That adoption curve has just popped into my mind," she goes on. "I can't tell an Early Majority nor a Late Majority person about this. They'll never listen to me. People like David Gushee might be allies in this kind of conversation transition."

"That is working out to be so in different ways. Look at the effect Gushee's book is having in the States. He got some real resistance and rejection for it from the hard right. But here's a blog which suggests some people can listen to him because they respect his other generally more right-wing views. For example, this blog's written by a guy who gave the Gushee book to his Dad." I read the short excerpt to her from my phone.

> Just for background my dad isn't an intellectual, but he is a committed Christian, always willing to throw himself into horrible situations to help comfort and witness to people. He always is willing to read things and loves to discuss faith with people of other religions and backgrounds.
>
> This morning he sent me the following:
>
> My Dad: Finished the book you gave me. You were right about him being someone I could relate to. I would definitely say my thinking has changed in many ways. I have always agreed with his take on respect & treatment of LBGTQ

folks but maybe not positions of authority in Church. I have made a lot of progress in that area as well.

Will pass the book along to [his pastor, who has a gay daughter as it happens] if you are still ok with that.

Me: I'm glad to hear it dad thanks. Go for it.

My Dad: Your Ma just found it on Kindle. I think she wants to read it as well. Based on my comments.[40]

"That's cool," says Charity, eyes gleaming.

I continue, getting my laptop open.

"I also found an article which includes comments from Gushee about the positive reception of his work and about some very wounding criticism.[41] In the first year after his book was published, he'd spoken widely by invitation, around the world, As well, he got heaps of criticism from the religious right. He's been elected president to two scholarly associations however, which shows scholarly approval of his work. Gushee is reported as saying: 'I've found that there's a large community of hurting people who are grateful that there is someone who gets what it's been like and is stepping forward as an ally.'"[42]

"Double cool," says Charity.

"Interestingly, there's comment from him on how church organisation affects the speed at which change can happen. Congregationally-gathered churches have more autonomy at the local level. Look at this piece here," I said.

I turn my laptop towards Charity and take the opportunity to go and get us second coffees. Charity leans forward and reads intently the section I'd highlighted:

> Americans who thought that evangelicals would be the last anti-gay crowd standing on the continent aren't aware of how evangelical, non-denominational and Pentecostal churches are organized. First, each believer looks to his or her relationship with God, largely through the pages of the Bible and prayer. Then, in discernment with other believers, congregations move forward.

In the current tidal wave of change in American attitudes toward LGBT men and women, Catholic lay people as a collective group already have shifted their viewpoint and so have United Methodists and other mainline Protestants. But, traditionally organized denominations require many years of debate, coupled with global consultation on their codes of church law. The Catholic and United Methodist denominations, as two prominent examples, simply cannot change their policies overnight – and perhaps not even after years of bruising debate on these issues.

However, if the Spirit is perceived to be moving, and if the biblical understanding is changing, thousands of evangelical churches across the U.S. can turn on a dime.

"It's the Protestant principle that every person is supposed to read the Bible for himself or herself, and is supposed to work things out with God," Gushee says. "I'm from a Baptist tradition and I can tell you: There's a lot of local autonomy in these kinds of congregations. These churches can pioneer – one by one – whatever they feel called by God to do. Every believer is on a journey with God and so is every congregation.

"Many of the non-denominational churches also are Baptist by design. They have local control. There's nobody above them. There's no hierarchy. That's where a lot of the energy has always been in evangelicalism and when change begins to happen – it can happen very rapidly. In this case, I see the change happening more quickly in younger institutions – meaning congregations where younger people are allowed to lead their churches in new directions.[43]

When I return to the table, Charity comments, "It's kind of like the difference between a tugboat towing a small boat compared with the difficulty of getting an ocean liner to turn around. I can see that as a problem for a nationally organised church. It has rules which need formal changes made to them with that two thirds majority. But our church is a really broad-based denomination with all sorts of views represented among parishes."

"Yes, and more documented tradition and history to work against," I agree as our caramel lattes arrive.

"But the protestant national churches must have changed since the reformation. What's that statement they keep on quoting?"

I quote, "the Church affirms *Ecclesia reformata, semper reformanda*, that is, 'the church reformed, always reforming', according to the Word of God and the call of the Spirit. That's right. But look at what it is believed should generate that change – the word of God and the Spirit. Two hefty hitters!"

"That's why Bible is so important. Even I know it's hard to convince people that a change is a movement of the Spirit and not just some crazy idea of people too young to know better!" Charity grins.

"Yes," I chuckle.

We fall silent, sipping the welcome coffee, appreciating its warmth and the energy of the caffeine kick. After a moment Charity muses out loud in a summing up kind of way.

"However, with the help of Gushee we have discovered that the First Testament references are based on patriarchal misogyny. They are prohibiting, as much as anything, violent sex, and sex outside formal relationships. There is also the question of how prescriptive First Testament rules are for post-Christ followers of Jesus."

"Then with Ed Oxford's help, we've discovered a huge mistranslation in Corinthians and Timothy. This leads to the conclusion that what is being prohibited there is adulterous sexual abuse and paedophilia."

"We haven't proved that only a man and a woman can get married in the eyes of God. We have argued however, that it's the quality of relationships which is the most important criteria as to whether a relationship should be regarded as sanctified or not."

"We've come a long way," I conclude.

"Yes, we have," says Charity.

"We've given authority a good shake by the scruff of the neck," I say. "Want to try out some of the arguments which liberals prefer? There's harm/care and fairness/justice and liberty/oppression in that group."

"What's the point? I already agree with those arguments."

"What if we spell out cogent rebuttals to the conservative view. Then see if we think, or your conservative friends think, they are convincing," I suggest.

"Good idea!" grins Charity. The light of challenge is in her eyes. "Let's do that next time, after I get my first assignments done for the semester."

We settle a time; she tugs the beanie back on and heads off to her lecture. It's time for us non-conservatives to put our arguments where our mouths are, or something like that.

8 – First do no harm

"I've been thinking about the argument which liberals favour most, the doing-no-harm one," says Charity as she settles into the booth the next time we meet, black felt trilby in place. She wears this hat when she means business. I notice she's drinking long black today too. Another sign of determination.

As usual, she'd finished her assignments at the last minute. Fortunately, she'd had a couple of days to unwind from the inevitable all-nighter she'd pulled at the end.

"What's come to mind?" I respond.

"I've been trying to remember that comment Jesus made about the Sabbath. He was being questioned by the scribes? I was given the impression they were trying to trap him into saying the wrong thing."

"I know the passage you mean. Let's pull up that chapter and see the full story." I tap and swipe my tablet screen and turn it to face Charity. "Here it is. It's in the Gospel of Mark, chapter two. See what's been put just before this story. First, Jesus heals that man who was let down from the roof."

"Oh, I loved that story when I was a kid. I loved imagining the bits of roof falling down on the crowd inside."

"I did too. What you may not have picked up on as a kid was that the most offensive thing Jesus did then was forgive the man's sins. That was when the scribes and Pharisees really thought he was going over the top."

I continue, "then the writer puts Matthew's call here with the comment that Jesus has come to be with those who need help, not those who don't. That's followed by his enigmatic comment that new wineskins are needed for new wine."

Charity nods. "It's all about things being different and new. It's about a new world really, isn't it? Where the teaching is for those who need it and will listen and about renewing our ideas of who might be carriers of the message."

"That's right. That's the context in which this comment of Jesus has been placed. See here."

> One Sabbath Jesus was passing through the grainfields, and His disciples began to pick the heads of grain as they walked along. So the Pharisees said to Him, "Look, why are they doing what is unlawful on the Sabbath?"
>
> Jesus replied, "Have you never read what David did when he and his companions were hungry and in need? During the high priesthood of Abiathar, he entered the house of God and ate the consecrated bread, which was lawful only for the priests. And he gave some to his companions as well."
>
> Then Jesus declared, "The Sabbath was made for man, not man for the Sabbath. Therefore, the Son of Man is Lord even of the Sabbath."[44]

"Is Jesus is saying rules are less important than human need?" asks Charity.

"I think he is." I reach for a napkin and draw it towards me, palming a pen at the same time.

"There was a network of rules which I grew up with in a fundamentalist church. This is the image which came to me." I draw a wire network shaped into a cube.

"Over the years the rules have come to form an unyielding and all-encompassing framework which traps people. What's more, the framework traps people in a shape which human beings were never intended to be. We weren't made to be all the same cube-sized stuff."

"This looks like one of those wire cages made to hold stones for landscaping work," says Charity, wrinkling her brow.

"Yes, here's a picture of some being used for that purpose." I quickly find the picture I'd accessed earlier on the tablet.

"Stones are firm and unyielding too, so they fit in the wire cages without damage to themselves, but if you try to cram people into such a confined place, they get damaged, hurt and deformed. It's interesting to reflect that you would need to curl up into a foetus position to fit in one of these. Psychologically speaking, assuming a foetal shape means you are young, unformed, able to be controlled because you are completely dependent. This kind of arrangement would work for any organisation trying to mould you to their ideas."

"Hmmm," murmurs Charity, her eyes filling with tears. "You know, this reminds me of the feelings I had when I was a teenager, trying to be brave enough to tell people who I was. It was really who I had always known I was, inside. There was pressure all around me to bend and fold in ways I didn't feel were right. When I was complying with what others wanted around me, I did feel squashed. And little. And powerless."

"That's where Jesus' comments and behaviour about the Sabbath are important," I reply.

"You mean 'the Sabbath was made for 'man', not 'man' for the Sabbath?'" Charity's 'speech marks' fingers were working overtime.

"Yes. The Sabbath is a very good idea. It's based on the myth of Creation where God took six days to make the world and on the seventh, as the story goes, God rested. That Sabbath rhythm was encouraged for all human beings. It was the original work/life balance, millennia before mindfulness became fashionable."

Looking puzzled, Charity asks, "so what does Jesus mean here?"

"By the time Jesus lived, Sabbath rest had become governed by heaps of rules. Anything which could be considered 'work' was banned on that day. There were lots of definitions of what work was. You could walk only a certain distance from your home. You could tie only certain kinds of knots. A woman could tie her rope girdle, but she couldn't tie a knot in the rope on a bucket to draw water from the well. The list became endless. An ordinary person had little hope of keeping them all."

"Is that what the disciples were doing in this story? Working? But they were just eating some grain!"

"Ah, but in doing so, they 'harvested' the grain. Pulling the ears of wheat off the stalk and rubbing them in their hands to get the kernel separated from the chaff would be all classified as work, so it was unlawful on the Sabbath."

Charity chuckles as she comments. "My great aunt told me when her great aunt was little, they weren't allowed to go to church with dirty shoes. But they were also not allowed to clean their shoes on Sunday morning. It all had to be done on Saturday night. They ate cold food on Sundays too which had been prepared the day before."

"The whole of New Zealand didn't do too much on Sundays right up to the start of Sunday trading in the 1980s. Conservative Christians were more rigid than others," I noted.

"My great aunt said she asked her great aunt if they didn't need to go to church if their shoes were still dirty on Sunday morning. Great Aunt Izzy just looked at her. She realised then there was no deviation allowed in the system at all. Church was a given, sabbath rest was a given, so cleaning your shoes on Saturday night was a given."

I nod. "That's the kind of rigidity with which the rules both in Jewish times and in Calvinist thinking could be kept. People fitted the rules. The rules did not bend to fit people. Never mind that people could worship perfectly well with dirty shoes."

Charity looks thoughtful. "I guess Jesus was saying there should be some give in the system. He would be saying you should get a rhythm of rest and work, keep life balanced, but that when unusual situations happened, the choice was in favour of the good of living things."

"Yes, a lot of people now work as hard on Sunday as they do any other day, and it does them no good. That's not what Jesus is meaning when he defends the disciples. But he is saying that the rules for the Sabbath should not be burdensome or confining."

"There's a distinction being made here, between these little, picky rules and wider values, isn't there?" says Charity slowly.

"There should be. This is what liberals mean when they argue against anything which harms people. Generally speaking, liberals put people first and rules second. The rules for them need to fit the people, not vice versa. That's the way Jesus thought. Otherwise, why would he say, 'I am come that they might have life and have it more abundantly'?[45] If you're really into rules, keeping that statement would seem very dangerous, as if the whole world was on a dangerous slide into chaos."

Charity nods. "One thing I notice between my family and my cousin's family is just that kind of approach. In Skye's family it's what her parents say and their rules which are most important. It's not that in my family we ignore Mum and Dad, but we know that if we break a rule or if we argue for a rule to be bent or put aside, we'll be listened to. Once we'd put our case, we knew our parents might well let us do the other thing, (if they were satisfied we wouldn't get harmed in any way)."

"Can you think of an example of that?" I ask.

"Mmm, let me think… I know! Skye's Mum had a firm rule that high school boy/girl relationships were 'out.' She had a friend whose daughter had formed a lasting relationship with a boy from school and got engaged right out of school and married quite young. Her friend was afraid the marriage wouldn't work out. Skye's Mum watched that and decided her daughters, (and Skye was the oldest), should not have a steady boyfriend while they were at high school."

"What happened next?"

"Skye did get around with a really nice boy in her middle years in high school. He was in the church youth group. I don't know how they kept it secret from Aunty Kirsty, because she was in charge of the youth group! Then it came out by accident, her Mum found out, and Skye was told to break it off."

"Did she?"

"Yes! They both went around looking unhappy for weeks. Mum even went to Aunty Kirsty and asked what they could do about these 'two unhappy young people.' Aunty Kirsty was offended. She saw it as intrusion into their family business."

"What do you think?"

"Well, Skye told me that she knew Kevin was going away to Med School in a distant city when he finished high school. She knew their 'relationship' wouldn't last past high school and couldn't see why her Mum couldn't see that. Skye was unhappy. So was he. He was embarrassed around Aunty Kirsty at church for a while. It seemed to me Aunty Kirsty just stuck to her rule and followed it whether or not it made her daughter unhappy, without wanting to hear any other sides of the story."

"What do you think your mother would have done had that been you?"

"She would have talked to me (again!) about the concept of not getting involved too deeply too young. She'd have told me (again!) why she thought that was a good idea. She would have asked how I saw things panning out. And listened. Then she would have said that she still thought it wasn't a great idea and to take it quietly."

Charity ponders for a moment longer, then grins cheekily.

"Then she would have made sure I was kept quite busy on things which didn't involve my boyfriend and when we were together, she'd have made sure we were always chaperoned!"

We laugh together. I know Charity appreciates her mother's love even more because she trusts her.

"I guess your Mum and Aunty Kirsty were setting their local family version of the Big Rule in fundamentalist churches. NO pre-marital sex and NO pregnancies outside wedlock."

"That would be right. I think the difference between my Mum and Aunty Kirsty was that Mum gave me good, detailed information about sex and boys and dating. According to Skye, Aunty Kirsty hardly talked about it. Probably didn't..."

"...want to put ideas into her head!"

We finish the sentence together, laughing as we do so. I was 25 years older than Charity, but mothers and daughters in conservative churches hadn't changed much!

"What would your Mum have done had you shown romantic interest then in a girl rather than in a boy?" I ask curiously.

Charity ponders my question.

"That's a really interesting point. Looking back now, she probably would have been more relaxed about it than I thought at the time. In my final year at school, she supported a bunch of us who wanted to go to the High School formal just as a group of girls. The principal and staff were amazingly picky about that. It was a bit of a struggle, but Mum and some of the other parents stood up for us."

"What did Skye do for the formal?"

"Oh, she came with us! I don't know if her Mum was relieved or disappointed."

"Relieved she wasn't going with Kevin, but disappointed she wasn't attracting a boy's attention?"

"Something like that!" We laugh again. Human beings are so inconsistent. We all contradict ourselves at least once a week!

"So how does this help us with our reasons based on harm/care?" I ask.

"Might need another cup before I answer that," replies Charity as she heads for the counter.

When she returns, she has a thoughtful look on her face. She reaches for a napkin and draws a line down the middle. That's where Charity and I differ. She always knows exactly where to find her pen. She looks up at me with a twinkle in her eye.

"I've turned into a version of you!" She starts writing words on either side of the line. On one side she writes 'Skye', 'Me', 'the gay community, human beings and their feelings'. Then she adds a title for the list – 'Bad'. On the other side of the line, she writes 'the rules', 'perfection', 'holiness', 'heaven', 'inhuman/ahuman' and at the top, alongside the 'Bad' title, she writes 'Good'.

"The dualisms we talked about earlier have interfered with how we see people," she says. She gestures with her pen towards the 'Good' list. "Some kind of good world, perhaps even a perfect world has been created in people's minds. They think it is the only way to be Christian." She adds the word 'Christian' to the 'Good' list.

"What we've ignored is that humans are humans. We're messy, chaotic creatures with unpredictable feelings. We don't all fit the same mould. All of that human messiness has been put on the 'Bad' list." She points to the list labelled 'Bad'.

"The rules become very important when you have a strong need to be on the 'good' list. But most people, left to themselves to choose what they really, really want and need, know exactly what that is.

They don't always choose those things selfishly, in a greedy envious kind of way. They mostly choose them because they know what is best for them."

"People aren't idiots. We know deep down what will make us truly happy in the sense of being completely fulfilled. You could call it that which will make us fully human. Sometimes our choices will coincide with the rules because the rules aren't all bad. They have wisdom and years of experience behind them – the 'big' rules I mean, the overarching values of love and mutuality and non-violence and honesty. But sometimes your heart's desire, what you truly need, does not comply with the little 'rules.' For your true happiness, you need to follow that heart's desire rather than lose it because of a 'little rule.'"

Charity stops, amazed, I think, at her own passion. I nod, knowing she isn't just talking about 'people' in general, but is thinking of her own coming out as lesbian. I keep quiet, though, and she continues.

"That's where banning lesbians and gays from the ministry or from having a same sex relationship is causing harm. It's not just being banned from those positions by the church, but it's the implicit message that acts like the confining metal cage you were talking about. It cramps and distorts and damages a gay person's image of themselves. It ruins their self-esteem and makes them second-guess themselves. No wonder the suicide statistics for gay young people are so high! Why would you want to continue living with a view of yourself like that? Why would you tolerate that hopeless feeling you will never come 'right' the way others want you to?"

Charity draws in a shaky breath and continues. "It's more than straight or gay, it's about how we view humanity. Are we just a bunch of selfish, greedy, and immoral animals or are we each sentient beings, able to think things through for ourselves? Are we able to tell what is best and able to discern for ourselves which rules are good and wholesome and wise, and which are just trying to manipulate and control us? This is what it is like to be human."

I go to speak, but Charity is on a roll.

"And! What right do we have, if we believe God created humans and saw that they were good, what right do we have to believe certain groups of humans are inherently bad?"

"When lists like this form in our heads and lodge in our guts," she waves her pen at the napkin lists she'd created, "when lists like this form, the self-proclaimed 'Good' side forgets, or never gets to know, how the others on the side they have called 'Bad' are thinking. What's more, they are not only ignorant about that, the 'Good' list people don't care if others see the world differently from them. That's when the harm starts, where the 'Bad' list people are expected to conform to the 'Good' list requirements no matter what. They're not given a voice; they're not listened to. They're regarded as second class. They're bad mouthed, mistreated and even killed."

Charity heaves a sigh which is more of a sob and reaches for another napkin, this time to wipe her eyes. I reach over to hug her, overwhelmed at her passionate, yet logical outburst.

Our church's national conference should hear her at full flow like this. Some living in a conservative bubble had not knowingly met a gay person. They didn't regard them as real people. I was reminded of Shylock's despairing cry in *The Merchant of Venice*, "If you prick us, do we not bleed? If you tickle us, do we not laugh? If you poison us, do we not die…?"[46] Those Other to the standard, white, patriarchal view of humanity, whoever they were – black skinned, gay, female, migrants – all had normal human reactions because they too were real human beings. We are all equally human.

I recall the next phrase in Shakespeare's script "…And if you wrong us, shall we not revenge?" The gay community had in a sense taken its revenge on the church by leaving it or never attending in the first place. This had ceased to surprise me though it was still a disappointment. Why should members of the gay community torture themselves by turning up to a church which had declared they were only partially acceptable? How much longer will Charity herself hang in with the church before she gives up in disgust at how she and other gay men and women are being treated?

Charity had dried her eyes while I was ruminating and sits quietly, still sniffing a little from time to time.

"Have you tried talking to your cousin Skye just this way?" I ask.

"Why do you ask that?" responds Charity.

"Well, we were going to see if your so-called 'liberal' arguments could persuade your fundamentalist cousin to a different point of view," I reply. "Are you close enough for you to be as direct with her? Do you think her experience with her mother over her high school boyfriend would help her to understand how it hurts when the rules are applied in an unyielding way?"

"Hmm," murmurs Charity. "I'll think about it."

She slowly packs up her things. Her outburst has taken a lot out of her. She looks tired, but also curiously peaceful. She reaches for the trilby and jams it on her ruffled hair.

"What's the theme next time?" she asks.

"Fairness and justice." I reply. "Today's topic and that are closely intertwined. Something which is not just or fair causes harm."

"Indeed!" she responds. She hefts her bag over her shoulder, giving me a wave as she pushes her way out the heavy swing door.

I watch her go, auburn hair flying out under that no-nonsense hat, with mixed feelings. Pride at her passion and resilience is mixed with sadness and pain that Charity could not live a carefree life, in which she knew she was seen by all others as just as acceptable as they saw themselves. Some words attributed to Jesus pop into my mind. 'Do to others as you would have them do to you.'[47] What if the gay community treated heterosexuals with disdain and prejudice? How would straight people feel then? Would they like it, if asked, as a T-shirt slogan I'd seen Charity wear put it, "When did you choose to become a heterosexual?"

Most gay people I talk to, both men and women, know from a very young age they are different from heterosexual siblings and friends. At first, maybe they hadn't worked out quite why, but it wasn't a 'choice' they displayed to the world in 'coming out.' Their coming out simply made public for the first time, an already existing identity which they had known within, in some fashion, for years.

My heart aches for Charity and other young lesbians and young gay men too. Their life is a lot more difficult because of their orientation. The Church purports to follow Jesus who urged his followers to treat everyone with the love they wanted themselves. Yet, ironically, the members of the gay community find being a member of the Christian community far more difficult. How could that be?

I go to the counter and order a third coffee, though I know a caffeine shot isn't going to fix the knot in my stomach.

9 – We're all equally human

I am first to get to *The Cup* the following week. Charity is due any minute. I look again at the dictionary entry I'd turned to on my laptop.

Justice:

just behaviour or treatment.

"a concern for justice, peace, and genuine respect for people"

The similar words listed beneath were an interesting mix:

Fairness, justness, fair play, fair-mindedness, equity, equitableness, even-handedness, egalitarianism, impartiality, impartialness, lack of bias, objectivity, neutrality, disinterestedness, lack of prejudice, open-mindedness, non-partisanship, honour, uprightness, decency, integrity, probity, honesty, righteousness, ethics, morals, morality, virtue, principle.[48]

Fascinating that many of the words, almost a third of them, were about fairness and lack of prejudice: "Fairness… equity, equitableness, even-handedness, egalitarianism, impartiality, impartialness, lack of bias … lack of prejudice, open-mindedness, non-partisanship," for example.

Frequently the word 'justice' was used in common speech to refer to whether a wrong doer was going to receive punishment, thereby gaining 'justice' for the victim. Sometimes, after a particularly horrifying murder or accident, relatives of the victims demand 'justice' loudly and with emotional heft.

In our country (and in church courts), however, the open-mindedness and even-handedness mentioned in the dictionary definition were valued. That was true even in apportioning blame or declaring the sentence on conviction. Courts were required to be objective in their dealings. When the meaning of the word justice is investigated, it is about treating people fairly whoever and whatever they were, not just about punishing people.

One unjust development of the gay-lesbian debate in the church was that if all the rules were followed to the last letter, no gay or lesbian minister or elder would ever attend our church's national conference. This meant the very group involved had no voice in their own future in the church. Increasingly, their friends and relatives also left the church in despair and concern. The numbers able to put the pro-argument were reducing every year.

In our secular legal system, those who could not afford a lawyer did have the option of legal aid representation. Even that kind of support was not offered to anyone with a same-sex orientation in the church. As I had said to Charity in an earlier conversation, this debate is dominated by emotions – fear, anger, and pain – not by objective, open minded, careful, and thoughtful debate.

When justice is referred to in the Bible, frequently it is as an aid to the disadvantaged. Take the prophet Isaiah: Learn to do right; seek justice. Defend the oppressed. Take up the cause of the fatherless; plead the case of the widow."[49] Justice is seen as a tool to relieve oppression of the weak. Orphans and widows fared badly in ancient society as the male was the protector. To be without a father or without a husband was to be at the very bottom of society, with no visible means of protection, no property, money, or food.

And in the famous Micah passage, the prophet pictures God as railing against the making of sacrifices and other obeisance towards God in favour of gifting to the divine something very simple and yet incredibly difficult:

> "He has told you, O mortal, what is good; and what does the Lord require of you? To do justice, and to love kindness, and to walk humbly with your God."[50]

This passage links justice with kindness and humility, not with subduing, punishing or ostracising others.

Then there was the woman caught in adultery who was brought to Jesus. He is urged to pronounce the sentence upon her, yet he suggests that if they were thinking of stoning her as the law required, that any person present who had never sinned should begin the stoning. Jesus bent down and started to write on the ground with his finger. When they kept on questioning him, he straightened up and said to them, "Let any one of you who is without sin be the first to throw a stone at her."[51] It is a very good comment. There's a pregnant pause. Then,

At this, those who heard began to go away one at a time, the older ones first, until only Jesus was left, with the woman still standing there. Jesus straightened up and asked her, "Woman, where are they? Has no one condemned you?" "No one, sir," she said.[52]

I love that the story, even in its edited form, describes that the older ones left first. Perhaps those with greater years and wisdom had the humility not to pretend or posture. How many of the ministers and elders who vote at national church conferences had never put a foot wrong in relationships? What kind of blameless life had they lived that they felt they could pass judgment on others? Especially how could they do that when there was increasingly evidence in the public domain that a gay relationship which was loving, mutual and non-violent was not banned by Scripture?

If we could see inside the Christian marriages represented at church conferences, would we always see enacted out the over-arching values Charity and I had discussed when we were talking about sanctity? They were more important than categorising people into sinful or not. How many of those heterosexual and therefore approved-by-the-church marriages were truly mutual in every aspect? How loving were those marriages after 25, 30 or more years of partnership? How non-violent were they? It is well known that domestic violence is not the preserve of the poor. Unfortunately, many affluent marriages and families are violent and abusive. How much scrutiny is focused on heterosexual relationships as practised by elders and ministers compared with the harsh spotlight turned on gay and lesbian pairings?

Even now when civil unions or same sex marriages are lawful in New Zealand, our church national conference still refused (narrowly) to change the rules affecting whether people in same sex relationships could be officially ordained as elders or ministers. Fairness and equity aspects of justice are not being honoured. A legal relationship is now open to the gay community, but the church will not study what that kind of public and legal commitment could mean.

Charity arrives with an apologetic air. "Sorry to be late," she says, "but I was arranging a weekend with Skye! She's coming to town next week. She's going to stay with me for a few days."

"That will be nice?" I question.

"Yes! We might be able to have a relaxed talk about rules and things in the process. She said she had something important to talk about with me, so I'm intrigued."

Charity is hatless today but as she takes off her jacket, I smile at the familiar T-shirt which asks, "When did you decide to become a heterosexual?" Snap! She grins back as she sees me smiling. "I could order a special job lot for the staff at the church if you like!" We laugh as we think of the rather staid musical director or the slightly portly senior minister wearing such a garment.

Charity's coffee arrives and she sips it appreciatively. "Ah! That's good. Now, what about justice!"

I share my thoughts with her about fairness and objectivity. She nods and looks carefully at the dictionary definitions on my laptop.

"Look," she says, "there's another group of words in here which suggest the more adjudicating, punishment angle. See?" She points out the words she means.

"Here, they're at the end of that list of similar words: 'honour, uprightness, decency, integrity, probity, honesty, righteousness, ethics, morals, morality, virtue, principle.' So, although the process of justice needs to be fair and open handed, and without bias or prejudice as you've been saying, justice is nevertheless about evaluating actions and people on grounds of morality and virtue, for example."

"Good spotting. What does that mean about how liberals and conservatives view justice as a concept?"

We both sip our coffee, thinking hard.

"Could it be," Charity begins tentatively "Could it be that liberals are more interested in fair play and people being treated equally. Do they think of that as justice – as just dealing – while conservatives see this other punitive side of justice more?"

"You mean conservative people think of justice more as moral judgments and righteousness and ethics?" I ask. "That's an interesting working theory. I did see a study which used Twitter feeds to analyse what conservative and liberal thinkers found most important in a 'good' society – which I would hope would be a just society also. This is their abstract."

I find the page I'd bookmarked and show Charity the screen. "Down here, see?"

> Liberals were more likely to raise themes of social justice, global inequality, women's rights, racism, criminal justice, health care, poverty, progress, social change, personal growth, and environmental sustainability, whereas conservatives were more likely to mention religion, social order, business, capitalism, national symbols, immigration, and terrorism, as well as individual authorities and news organizations. There were also some areas of convergence: Liberals, moderates, and conservatives were equally likely to prioritize economic prosperity, family, community, and the pursuit of health, happiness, and freedom.[53]

"That doesn't quite speak to your suggestion, but it does indicate that liberals and conservatives approach the goodness or justness of a society from different angles."

"So…," says Charity reflectively, "in the church conference debate, liberals argued for justice to be done by treating gay and straight people the same. Conservatives do not see that as just. Because they believe the Bible says homosexuality is a sin, they see justice being done by 'punishing' or excluding homosexuals from positions of leadership. Huh. We were talking past each other. Even using the same word, we mean different things."

I nod. "According to this abstract, in any church debate, the conservative view would be concerned about religion (i.e. what the Bible says), social order (i.e. following Church rules and moral codes), and individual authorities (i.e. what your local minister or eldership thinks)."

"Look at the end of the abstract, This article says both sides have in common – 'prosperity, family, community' and, ironically the 'pursuit of health, happiness and freedom!' I doubt whether any of these church debates, however well conducted and however polite people are, leave people feeling healthy, happy and free on either side."

We both sit silent for a moment. The irony was almost too much to bear. In the end I break the silence.

"So, while we haven't done an exhaustive survey on it, it seems likely that the different sides of this debate do think differently about justice. When liberals ask for equal treatment in the church, that probably offends conservatives because they do not want to condone what they see as wrongdoing. They don't want to treat a chronic and intentional wrongdoer the same as someone who has, in their eyes, always done the right thing."

"And," I add, "of course, when someone is in a gay relationship, to a conservative that looks like the person is an unreformed and obdurate criminal, intending to keep on 'sinning' as they see it."

"It really does show that the key issue is the authority of the Bible," I conclude. "If people can't see that the acts which are condemned in the Bible are aberrant and abusive, and that the Bible is not condemning relationships which are mutual and loving, between consenting adults, then they will continue to resist equal treatment of gay people in the church."

Charity heaves a heavy sigh and sits silently, digesting my words. I continue.

"Another article I found deals with varying approaches to social justice between the two groups. It points out the flattering and unflattering aspects of each approach to social justice. One difference is a greater empathy and understanding of the disadvantaged group by liberals, compared with ability by conservatives to see that a wider time frame, delaying help now, might benefit people in the long run. It also points out that the 'bleeding heart' syndrome which liberals are accused of is true. Again, it's not quite the same topic, but suggests very different ways of thinking and varying inner psychological orientations. All of this is in the mix."

I add, "this may mean that when we link harm/care with fairness/justice, that one side cannot see as clearly when disadvantage becomes harmful, while the other sees it all too clearly and becomes emotional and passionate which skews their ability to argue logically and clearly. Each side of the argument has its Achilles' heel."

"This is really illuminating," says Charity, "though I wish I wasn't one of those liberals who feels the pain! This shows why it is important that people meet 'real live gay people' and get to know them as human beings." Again, her fingers indicated the speech marks obvious in her tone of voice.

"That's right," I agree. "Some people can imagine themselves in another's shoes, but others need concrete evidence of the pain this is causing individuals and families. That's not always visible if the damage is being caused internally, in the mental space. For instance, if a farmer sees a sheep not doing well, they feed or treat it and make sure it recovers to full health and vitality. If a sheep is feeling 'ashamed' inside, there's often no outer evidence of that, so the farmer may not react. That would be basic animal welfare – you can often only treat what you see."

"Just coming out in regular society is hard enough because society has its conservative elements which don't like difference from the norm to which they are accustomed. Any minority has a hard time in any society, however secular or liberal it might be. They encounter all the fear and unconscious emotion people reserve for what is different or unusual or a surprise."

"Exactly," says Charity. "So, shouldn't gay people find a refuge from that prejudice and fear in the church? Of all places, shouldn't they find acceptance there?"

"You're preaching to the choir! Of course, they should. Of all places. What is Jesus reported as saying in Matthew? I remember it best in the King James Version which is how I learned it as a child."

> Come unto me, all ye that labour and are heavy laden, and I will give you rest.
>
> Take my yoke upon you and learn of me; for I am meek and lowly in heart: and ye shall find rest unto your souls.
>
> For my yoke is easy, and my burden is light.[54]

"It follows a tirade that Jesus has just delivered against cities where he was not welcomed or acknowledged. He has just recalled that they called him a glutton and a drunkard because he ate with people who were not following kosher rules. Then these words are placed at the end, with an alternative view of how things could be. Alternatively, a leader might gently lead the people, like a considerate farmer might gently lead oxen under their yoke as they pull a burden which will never be too heavy to bear."

Charity's sigh this time is heartfelt and peaceful.

"Thank you. I needed to hear that." She sighs again. "I've always loved that piece. Even more so when I read how it's paraphrased in

The Message. I've saved it on my phone so I can read it any time. Listen…" she scrolls through her phone.

> "Are you tired? Worn out? Burned out on religion? Come to me. Get away with me and you'll recover your life. I'll show you how to take a real rest. Walk with me and work with me – watch how I do it. Learn the unforced rhythms of grace. I won't lay anything heavy or ill-fitting on you. Keep company with me and you'll learn to live freely and lightly."[55]

"'unforced rhythms of grace…' I love that. Well, I must be going. How about we meet up after Skye's visit? I can debrief you on whether or not I manage that conversation with her."

"All the best for that. Just be yourself. Take it easy tonight too. It's been a rough session today," I reply with a wan smile.

She gives me an equally wan smile and is out the door.

I recall again Shylock's heartfelt cry 'If you prick us do we not bleed?' Jesus' offer of 'rest unto your souls' and the 'unforced rhythms of grace' sounds pretty good about now.

10 – Let my people go

While I wait for Charity the next week, I check definitions for oppression on my tablet. I use the word reasonably often but am curious to know what nuances an official definition would include. Many similar words appear in my online dictionary.[56]

n: oppression; plural noun: oppressions

1. prolonged cruel or unjust treatment or exercise of authority.

   • the state of being subject to oppressive treatment.

   • mental pressure or distress.

Similar words: persecution, abuse, maltreatment, ill treatment, tyranny, despotism, repression, suppression, subjection, subjugation, enslavement, exploitation, cruelty, ruthlessness, harshness, brutality, injustice, hardship, misery, suffering, pain, anguish, wretchedness.

Opposite words : freedom, democracy. [57]

The Google search throws up a short quote from Wikipedia.

Oppression is malicious or unjust treatment or exercise of power, often under the guise of governmental authority or cultural opprobrium. Oppression may be overt or covert, depending on how it is practiced.[58]

As I mull over this quote, I think about the New Zealand government's previous longstanding treatment of homosexuality as illegal, punishable by dire penalties.

'Cultural opprobrium' takes many forms. Being the butt of jokes as a 'different' group in society takes its toll after a while. How many times did you have to laugh when your kind of person was being ridiculed, or worse, abused and vilified? I knew most women were tired of 'dumb blond' jokes, for example.

My attention lingers on the last sentence in the quote. Overt, oppressive speech and actions are now often throttled back and might disappear. But, what about covert oppression where gay people quietly found it harder to get jobs, rent homes or get bank loans because of their minority lifestyle?

Different kinds of oppression stand out for me in the Bible. The Exodus experience was a biggie. Over centuries Jewish people had fled to Egypt to find refuge and jobs and food. They had become a problem to the Egyptian rulers over time, especially as their population grew relative to the Egyptian population. The story suggests Egyptian rulers were afraid of what such a large migrant population could do. It is a familiar scenario in our contemporary world. Large numbers of migrant groups fearing oppression and war in their homelands put pressure on the countries to whom they flee.

In ancient Egypt, enslavement and back breaking, soul-destroying work were devised, to trap the Hebrew people into a bondage from which they could seemingly never escape. Is oppression of the gay community in some countries today similar to the treatment of the Hebrews, albeit more subtle. Who would call 'let my people go' in this scenario?

Look at Western history. Oscar Wilde was a notable homosexual playwright of the 19th century when homosexuality was illegal in Britain. He was imprisoned for two years hard labour under those laws, after which he exiled himself in France. He died there, ill and in poverty. Yet his witty plays are produced and re-produced by theatre companies all over the world to the delight of many audiences, gay and straight. His volatile and creative personality could be said to have been oppressed, "under the guise of governmental authority or cultural opprobrium."

As of the early 2000s, oppression of the LGBT community, and individuals within it, have been little studied.

> Lesbian, gay, bisexual, and transgendered (LGBT) people continue to experience various forms of oppression and discrimination in North America and throughout the world, despite the social, legal, and political advances that have been launched in an attempt to grant LGBT people basic human rights. Even though LGBT people and communities have been actively engaged in community organizing and social action efforts since the early twentieth century, research on LGBT issues has been, for the most part, conspicuously absent within the very field of psychology that is explicitly focused on community research and action – Community Psychology.[59]

At the same time, another life study showed there was unequal treatment in fields of health provision especially mental health treatment in rural areas, despite claims of the opposite from providers. This shows that overt neutrality masks covert bias in real-life situations.

> **Results:** A majority of rural providers claimed that there is no difference between working with LGBT clients and non-LGBT clients. This neutral therapeutic posture may be insufficient when working with rural LGBT clients. Despite providers' claims of acceptance, lack of education about LGBT mental health issues, and homophobia influenced services for rural LGBT people. LGBT clients had been denied services, discouraged from broaching sexuality and gender issues by providers, and secluded within residential treatment settings.[60]

Research into rainbow related issues has been carried out in New Zealand too. A Massey University senior lecturer in social work has published *Lavender Islands: Portrait of the Whole Family*, a study he has been working on since 2004. This is, "the first national, strengths-based study of New Zealand's lesbians, gays and bisexuals."[61]

> New Zealand lesbian, gay and bisexual Christians have quit mainstream religion at two-and-half times the rate of the general population, according to a Massey University study.

> "Christian religions by and large have done an excellent job in communicating that a Christian identity and a homosexual identity are incompatible, or at least difficult to reconcile," says report author Dr Mark Henrickson.

> "A large number of raised Christians appear to have resolved the dissonance between their identities and their religion by leaving their religion."

The study researched more than just church attendance, but about attendance in organised religion, the researcher comments:

> Of the 2269 participants in the survey, 73 per cent said they were raised as Christians, with 22.5 per cent not raised in any religion. But only 15 per cent of raised Christians were currently practicing their religion, while 73 per cent of the gay, lesbian and bisexual participants were currently non-religious. Buddhism, Islam, Hinduism and "other" religions accounted for only a small percentage of responses.

The difference between the 73 per cent raised Christian and the 15 per cent who are currently Christian "is a remarkable 80 per cent decline," Dr Henrickson says.

He compared the figures to those of the 2001 census, which revealed that people identifying themselves as Christian dropped from 90.1 per cent to 59.8 per cent – a decline of 33.6 per cent in 35 years when compared with figures from the 1966 census.

The results of the study showed that "for most people, if they are forced to make a choice between their religious faith and their personal identity, they'll choose their personal identity."

"What we can say is that whatever negative messages that organised religions want to communicate – they're working."

"They're not working to change gay people, they're working to drive them away," says Dr Henrickson, who is himself an Anglican priest, but stresses he is not speaking in his role as a clergyman.[62]

This has been my own impression of the debate in my own church. Eagerness to follow the 'right' moral standards has been alienating rainbow communities and their straight friends and family since at least 1991. Even in gay-friendly local parishes, it is difficult to ignore that the national church, of which the local parish is a part, has a less friendly view.

Peter Lineham, MNZM is a prominent historian of religion in New Zealand who later in life has gone public with his gay identity.[63] Fellow New Zealand historian of religion, Allan Davidson ONZM notes that,

In coming out as a gay man, Peter has had to deal with the pain of exclusion and opposition from some within his own church community and the Evangelical world. Uniquely, Peter currently participates and gives leadership in 'a Baptist, an Anglican and a gay church.' He admits that this 'is pretty whacky and makes my Sundays very busy. The simple fact is that my background has led me to appreciate that small religious movements actually play an unusually influential role in the shaping of community.'[64]

While Lineham's gay identity has not resulted in copious historical writing of his own on the rainbow community's relationship with organised religion, he does comment in *Sunday Best* that while "the gender culture of local churches has always reflected wider social trends," the church has "been slow and cautious to treat gender and sexualities as equals."[65]

Scrolling through the archives of the news section on my phone I find my memory is accurate. It is correct that the New Zealand government increased funding to rainbow groups for mental health issues early in 2021. Comments made by the prime minister on announcing the funding show society is starting to notice the greater problems in mental health which the LGBT community experiences because of prejudice and discrimination – the covert 'cultural opprobrium' of my online definition.

The Government is providing \$4 million to services that provide mental health support to young members of New Zealand's Rainbow community.

> "The Government is committed to improving mental health outcomes for children and young people in our Rainbow communities," Ardern said.
>
> *"Young people in the Rainbow community are at greater risk of being discriminated against, bullied and harassed. As a result, they have poorer physical and mental health and addiction outcomes and are at greater risk of suicide. We need to change that."*
>
> *"Participants in the Counting Ourselves survey who are trans or non-binary were twice as likely to have attempted suicide in the past year than participants who did not report that discrimination."*
>
> *Ardern added the move was a "long overdue commitment to some of our most vulnerable youth"...*[66]
>
> Most of the money – \$3.2m – will be used to expand mental wellbeing services focusing on young Rainbow New Zealanders. The rest will top up the existing Rainbow Wellbeing Legacy Fund, which was established as an acknowledgement of those New Zealanders who were convicted for homosexual acts before the law was changed in 1986. The total package will be spread over four years.[67]

It is over 30 years since the Homosexual Law Reform Act, yet this article's reference to the Wellbeing Legacy Fund indicates that the results of oppression, especially when enshrined in law, have long lasting effects. Mark Beehre's photo essay *A Queer Existence*[68] describes and shows the lives of 27 young homosexual men born since the passing of the Law Reform Act. In a radio interview promoting the book's publication, Mark names the low self-esteem which still lingers, despite the oppressive illegality having been lifted.[69]

A transwoman friend first introduced me to the Transgender Day of Remembrance (TDOR) held in November of each year. The annual lists of victims provided for this day – trans men and women who are raped, assaulted, and killed – are shocking. Hundreds of men and women in countries throughout the world are listed, along with the inevitable comment that this list probably doesn't represent the true numbers involved. Contrary to scary reputations given to transgendered individuals by disapproving cis individuals, it is obvious the trans community is an extremely vulnerable group.

One legal barrier for this group is gender information required for legal identification such as passports and drivers licences. Formal recognition in public legislation that you exist is a means of beginning to alleviate oppression, neglect, and ignorance. Australia is thought to be the first country to allow a so called 'third gender' passport in 2003 in response to a specific case. Another followed in Australia in 2014. New Zealand has offered a third classification of gender since 2012 using the letter X, though passports denoting indeterminate sex for intersex people were available previously. Sixteen countries outside the United States are described as offering varying positions on legal recognition of a 'third' gender. Some states in the USA are also making this available. The first US ruling allowing a transgender man to be recognised as non-binary in gender is claimed to be in 2016 in the state of Oregon.

Beginning with Australia in 2003, an increasing number of legal recognitions has occurred in other jurisdictions in the past decade. Despite New Zealand's third gender classification, going through security checks at airports can turn out to be humiliating, especially for transpeople, even when body scanners are used.[70]

Legal changes on behalf of national and state governments are a lifting of legal oppression. It is a moot point whether the general 'cultural opprobrium' displayed by regular people changes more or less quickly than these legal changes. After this overt oppression is lifted, does covert oppression still operate daily for transgender and intersex people? Judging from the heightened suicide rates cited by New Zealand Prime Minister in early 2021, trans and non-binary youth do not feel comfortable with life as it is for them currently. This despite New Zealand having an image of itself as relatively enlightened.

An email from Charity interrupts my train of thought. She's got a rare appointment with the Head of the Psych Department and needs to cancel, with her apologies. Her email has a new quote in the signature: "The only choice I made was to be myself." I smile. I know why that's appeared!

I reply 'OK, no problem' and continue to muse. In a sense I'm glad Charity's not here. As a member of the rainbow community, these discussions are hard on her. Recognising and teasing out the degree of oppression which the LGBTQI community experienced doesn't constitute a fun day for her.

There are differences between 'church' and 'society.' I can see that if church people feel homosexuality in all its forms is contrary to Christian scriptures, then they will be wary, suspicious and downright rejecting of those thought to 'sin' in this way. This was especially true in respect to ongoing homosexual or lesbian relationships, which may be seen by homophobic conservatives as 'premeditated sin.'

Why, though, was general society so wary and suspicious? Was it the generally pervasive effect of Christianity throughout the whole of western society? Did people follow this line of oppressive reaction because they or their forebears had been imbued with the Christian prohibitions learned from mistranslations and poor biblical interpretation?

Or is it those pesky lists of ethical dualisms which pervade the whole of western society? Is it simple, but widespread misogyny that led to first, disdain for gay men, and then to anger against lesbians for not seeming to 'need' men? That didn't require a religious upbringing to be a motivation out of which unreflective people might react.

It was probably 'both/and.' I'm not enjoying the line my thoughts are taking. Perhaps in the same way the word sinister became known as tricky or devious when it originally only meant left-handed. A man in medieval times could be fatally surprised by an opponent wielding a sword from an unexpected direction, so left-handed people – sinister people – were associated with cunning and deviance. Perhaps in the same way powerful men over the centuries had been blindsided by another man's sexual orientation or surprised at rejection from a lesbian woman. This could result in discomfort and unease when interacting with LGBTQI individuals, even in routine business management and governance.

You could add the tendency to an acerbic and sharp-edged wit which I notice in some members of the rainbow community. For straight and cis people, this somewhat black humour is disconcertingly blunt about homosexual and heterosexual difference. It springs out of the ill treatment and disdain the gay community encounters, but also often, I imagine, could have the effect of rendering people who had hitherto thought they 'ruled the world,' ill at ease and resentful of being made to feel that way.

Personally, I enjoy that sharp edged humour. There are many ways in which heterosexual society needs to be called out about its assumptions of entitlement and dominance. It is good for straight people to be urged to look at themselves in a new light.

It's always a shock though, when a group you'd previously undervalued proves to have ideas, values and a sense of humour you don't expect. More of a shock when the sense of humour was directed at you!

Even without active discrimination and prejudice or abuse, members of the rainbow community seldom find themselves in a world where their lifestyle, humour, experience, and family structures are the majority. It didn't need straight people to be nasty for a society where heterosexual images and metaphors predominate, to suggest, without words, that you are unusual and different. Most real estate brochure advertisements show houses with straight family members. 'Family' usually means a mum and dad and children, and when the word couple is used, it mostly refers to a guy and a girl, not two guys or two girls.

New Zealand libraries should have gay and lesbian sections where the rainbow community can easily find literature which depicts their lives. No one needs to be overtly nasty or violent for anyone to get the message that being gay is the minority orientation and therefore automatically suspect to others. Covert opprobrium indeed.

It was no wonder that the 'out and proud' message had been common in latter years, along with Gay Pride parades where 'anything went' in costuming and actions. While these events repel some, it is obvious many straight New Zealanders enjoy the vivacity and energy of these celebrations. In pre-covid pandemic times, they lined the streets for Gay Pride parades and attended fairs and 'Out in the Park' events. The generally less exuberant majority of straight people, take a vicarious delight in the colour and creativity which Pride events openly display. It seems wrong a mixed message was the result. 'Entertain us,' society seems to say, 'but don't think we count you as one of us completely.'

Oppression takes many forms. Some are disguised with colour, humour, and tokenism but they damage people, nevertheless. The Church should have no truck with any form of oppression of any kind of group, any time, any place, anyhow.

11 – The umbrella may be colourful, but it needs to be wide

[**CW//** Talk of dysphoria, body image and appearance: pp. 102-104, 106, 107.]

Charity emails the week after her cousin's weekend visit, arranging time and place. She ends with a tantalising "What till you hear what I've got to tell you!" followed by several emojis expressing shock and awe.

We meet the following Thursday, arriving in the door of *The Cup* at the same time. We order at the counter together, exchanging comments on the weather, (which is unseasonably cold), and on Charity's hat this week, a squashy cap with deep brim, a glorious patchwork creation in rainbow colours.

I am bursting with curiosity but hold back on the questions while we're in the queue. At last, we are in our usual booth. "Well, spill," I say, leaning forward.

"Well…!" says Charity with a twinkle in her eye.

"Well?"

"You know Skye was here last weekend. She'd told me she had something to fill me in on, so I was agog. It took a while for her to warm up, but eventually she blurted out that she's going to come out to her family this week on her 21st birthday weekend."

"Come out?" I repeat stupidly.

"Not coming out like I came out. I thought it was that at first. I started to tell her it wasn't as bad an experience as I had feared. But she interrupted and said she wasn't a lesbian. She's going to come out to her parents as non-binary!"

"Really?" It is all I can think of to say. This is so unexpected. Compassion for Skye wells up inside me as I think of her introducing this no doubt foreign concept to her fundamentalist parents.

"It's true! Skye said she'd never felt very comfortable as a girl. She did always do a lot of tomboy things around the farm, but I thought that was kind of how a lot of farm girls act. She said, though, she always had a deeper disconnect inside. It wasn't just adjusting to 'girls can do anything' or being gay or being a kind of butch type of woman which would fix that. She really feels uncomfortable trying to be totally female."

"How did she come across non-binary as a solution?"

"She's been searching the internet for a long time. Then, when she went to teacher training college, she roomed with someone who knew a lot about the gay scene. They had long talks, and she slowly noticed others around campus using 'they' and 'them' as pronouns and wearing more androgynous clothing which she prefers too. She wants everyone to use 'they' and 'them' as pronouns for her. So, I should do that from now on, I keep forgetting."

"It is hard using 'they' and 'them' isn't it?" I responded. "You feel you're suddenly addressing a crowd of people. A friend of mine suggested using 'tis' and 'eim', but terms need to arise naturally. Remember the rocky start that 'Ms' had in the 1980s?"

Charity looks blank. Of course, she is too young to remember that.

"Yes I do find it difficult using 'they/them', but I need to, to support Skye. It's still new for them but they thought they would practise on me before telling their parents. Skye's really scared but determined."

"How do you feel about all this?" I ask.

"Well, actually apart from the shock of being totally surprised, I found Skye knows more about the non-binary scene than me. I've focused on what being lesbian means, so I'm not as familiar with the rest of the letters in the rainbow umbrella. What are they up to now? It used to be LGBTQI."

"I was checking the other day, as it happens. You could use LGBTQQIP2SAA! How's that? It stands for lesbian, gay, bisexual, transgender, questioning, queer, intersex, pan-sexual, two-spirit (2S), androgynous and asexual."

"There was a shorter list being used till recently, wasn't there?" asks Charity, a little overwhelmed by my offering.

"Yes, the more usual is LGBTQI, sometimes with a question mark as in LGBTQI? The rainbow umbrella covers many different groups which vary greatly in their key characteristics. I'm getting to understand more about those differences as I meet more diverse members of the rainbow community."

"Like I said, each letter group doesn't always know much about the other's situations, either," responds Charity. "You know that famous lesbian minister who did so much work in the secular community defending the gay position? Someone asked her about transgender issues. She said she didn't know much about them at all. It wasn't because she wasn't interested, but it takes all her energy to work on the issues she confronts associated with her orientation. That's how it's been for me too."

"Heterosexuals do assume that each person in the rainbow community is like all the others in the rainbow community. Many have no idea of the diversity underneath that umbrella. It's a bit like Palangi New Zealanders assuming all Pacific Islanders all act the same way, know each other well, and like each other!"

"Another case of the Good list people assuming the Other is a homogeneous, monochromatic, monolithic group," retorts Charity. There's heat in her tone and her eyes flash greenly.

"That's right. One major difference between the groups under the rainbow umbrella (which needs to be giant golf umbrella size!) is that it began with the main groups attracting attention for their sexual orientation – gay men, lesbian women, bisexual people. The issues with them were that they, as men and women, were partnering with the same sex or both sexes which was not the usual in our mainly heterosexual society. But in those groups of people, everyone generally knew who was a male and who was a female. The problem for rule-following-heterosexuals was that gays and lesbians were not following the sexual rules which straight society had set down."

"So if those three letters represent sexual orientations, what do the rest represent?" asks Charity.

"The remaining letters are mostly about sexual identity – am I male or female or something else? The life experience of people represented by the letters T, Q and I call into question what a male is and what a female is, and whether those categories are enough to cover the lived experience of all people," I respond.

"Ok," muses Charity, "so the T is for transgender. That's say, a man or a woman who does not feel their birth gender or assigned gender is their felt sexual identity. Inside they feel more male than their female body would suggest to onlookers, or they feel more female than their male-looking body would suggest. That's right? Do members of the T for trans group always have surgery and hormone treatment?"

"It varies with the person and how far they are on their transition. At one end of the spectrum, you could have what are often called cross dressers, where the person wears the clothes of the opposite sex, but haven't done anything about hormone treatment or surgery."

"I guess that's for them to know. It's not really anyone else's business what, if any, treatment people have had," Charity comments.

"Exactly. The good thing about treatment is that it often includes some counselling or at least a talk with your doctor and other medical people so the person gets a chance to discuss the implications. But for those conversations to be helpful, the medical people need to be on board with the issues."

I continue, "I was very struck the other day to hear a trans man say that for them coming out is simply letting others know what they themselves have known all their lives. We've talked about that in other connections. It's not news to them but is news to other people who have just assumed they are like most heterosexual people. The term for that strong feeling of not being 'right' as the world sees them is gender dysphoria. It just doesn't 'fit' for them to be what the world thinks they are. This is bigger than 'girls can do anything,' as Skye found."

I thought of something else and continued

"Recently I met a trans man whom I had known years ago as a woman. I'd been around when she was beginning her transition. I even created and led a ritual for her to symbolically make the transition with her friends. I realised a little too late that quite a few of her friends were gob-smacked and not entirely approving! It was all moving too fast for them. It was a slightly awkward day, but I hope the ritual helped a little."

"When I met him again the other day, I was struck by how 'happy in his skin' he is now as a man. He's lived as trans for some years now. The woman I had known had been prickly and bit reactionary. No wonder, now I know what was going on for her at the time. Now he is self-assured and relaxed, though I'm sure life is still tricky occasionally given general ignorance about such things." I smile, remembering Alan's happiness that day, then carry on.

"Georgina Beyer is a trans woman who became publicly successful after her transition. She was a local mayor, then a member of Parliament as well. There are not many publicly known examples though. Have you noticed when a woman becomes a trans male it doesn't cause many waves, but when a man becomes a trans woman, it attracts much more flak? Sexism raises its ugly head again!" I say wryly.

"It's the same misogynistic reaction of which gay men are the focus. I guess really macho men can't imagine a man wanting to be a woman unless he was defective in some way!" Charity retorts. We both laugh. Again, had we not laughed, we would have cried.

"Moving on," says Charity. "There are a few more letters to go. I think we need more coffee. I'll get it. Two cappuccinos this time? "

While she's placing our orders, I refresh my information on New Zealand websites which focus on educating people about rainbow vocabulary. Insideout[71] has very good resources aiming at educating staff, students, and families of high school pupils. I'm scanning their list of rainbow terminology[72] as Charity returns from the counter. I turn the tablet screen towards her.

"See here, Q can stand for 'queer' or 'questioning'. This resource says

> Queer: A reclaimed word that is often used as an umbrella term encompassing diverse sexualities and genders. It can also be used as an individual identity for someone who is either not cis-gender or not heterosexual and is often preferred by people who describe their gender or sexuality more fluidly.[73]

"I need to ask about cis-gender," responds Charity, "but let's stay with 'queer' for now. I see it's called a reclaimed word. What's that mean?"

"Like the black movement in the States reclaimed 'black' as a badge of pride during the civil rights uprising in the 1960s. In the USA in 1979 I felt uncomfortable calling people black, but it was more of an insult to call them negroes, because of its associations with other 'n' words. Being black was becoming a source of pride and a rallying call."

"'Queer' is the same," I continued. "It used to be used as an insult. But it's been picked up and used consciously as a countermovement to that prejudice. You'll see here this term is not about who you are oriented or attracted to, but about your own identity. From a gender point of view, 'queer' gives people space."

Charity nods, her face thoughtful. "This will all have come through in recent years following the renewed interest in gender being a social construct. Whether we are male or female or something else has been taught us as much as anything by the way our society behaves and the norms and customs in which we have been socialised."

"Yes," I affirm.

"So, someone calling themselves queer, might be gay or lesbian, but more likely these days are telling us that they want to be fluid about their gender identity?" asks Charity.

"Yes. It's a relatively new development where a person, when they sign anything or write a CV, may list the pronouns they would prefer to be used to describe them, like your cousin Skye told you their pronouns. A male would use 'he' or 'him' while a queer person, especially one wanting to be recognised as non-binary, would use 'they' or 'them.' It's a bit tricky because using 'they' or 'them' suddenly seems to suggest a crowd rather than an individual. On the other hand, perhaps that's what they are saying: 'I am more than only an individual female or an individual male, I am more than one.'"

"That makes sense when you put it that way. What about cis-gender? I never heard that before." Charity points to the word on the screen.

"That was a new one on me too. That's amusing because it refers to both of us. We were born female and are happy to live as females. Anyone who remains with the gender identity into which they were born is 'cis.' It is the opposite to 'trans.' What does the online dictionary say? 'Referring or relating to people whose sense of personal identity and gender corresponds with their birth sex. Cis-gender'"[74]

"We are both 'cis,' though I'm gay and you're straight? I guess a bisexual woman would be cis too?"

"Yes, same gender identity but different orientations. If their sex at birth was female, then a straight woman, a bisexual woman and a lesbian woman are all 'cis-gender'. It's the same with men, a straight man, a bisexual man and a gay man who were born male are also cis-gender."

"This must be very hard to explain to older people for whom life has always been binary when it comes to gender," comments Charity. "In my grandparent's time, you were a man, or you were a woman, and there were no variations in between. Or, if there were, they were seen as freaks."

"That's right," I agree. "That's particularly the case, unfortunately, with our next letter, I. I stands for intersex. This is a different group again. The old word for this group was hermaphrodite because they are often physically born with either male genital organs in what seems otherwise to be a female body or vice versa or some combination of that. In some cases, they are truly (scientifically speaking) hermaphrodite as they have organs of both sexes. This is that kind of situation where parents or medical staff 'assign' a gender to the baby – of course not knowing then how the grown child or adult would want to be – and it can turn out badly. Intersex individuals have a gender identity issue thrust upon them by their physical body from birth."

"Wow." Charity is obviously surprised. "I suppose too that they will probably be different from the 'loud and proud' image which the rainbow community has. That must be an extremely personal and difficult situation to be in. You're not necessarily going to want to go public and face all the embarrassing and intrusive questions you will get."

I nod. "That's right. Mani Bruce Mitchell is a role model for intersex individuals in New Zealand. Recently Mani is quoted as being amazed at seeing 'intersex people moving out of that shame and secrecy and into a playful, joyful place over the years.' That was when Mani became a member of the Order of Merit in the 2021 Queen's Birthday Honours list, the first intersex person to get such an honour. Notice the pronoun used in the caption under Mani's picture here: "Mani Bruce Mitchell has been made a Member of the New Zealand Order of Merit for their services to the intersex community, particularly in the areas of education and advocacy."[75] See the use of 'their' where if Mani was a woman, it would have been 'her' or if Mani was a man, it would have been 'his.' The article goes on."

> Having been wrongly identified at birth in 1953 as a hermaphrodite, Mitchell later trained as a counsellor and is considered one of the first people in New Zealand to publicly come out as intersex. They had non-consensual genital "feminising" surgeries when they were younger, and they are also a survivor of sexual abuse.
>
> Mitchell has contributed to initiatives to help include intersex conditions in the fields of mental health, sexual health and medicine. People may also recognise them from the award-winning documentary *Mani's Story*, or from narrating the 2012 film *Intersexion*, which is used as an educational resource by the United Nations Commission on Human Rights.[76]

"Wow. I must look up those films and that article," exclaims Charity.

"Mani is amazing. I remember them being incredible busy with the number of people they were supporting through counselling and the community work they did."

"This bit here is interesting," says Charity still poring over the article.

> Intersex people have innate sex characteristics that don't fit medical norms for typical female or male bodies, which create risks and experiences of stigma, discrimination and harm. "We have many different kinds of bodies and life experiences," Mitchell said.[77]

"And look here," Charity adds. "Mani found Māori attitudes to intersex children are different from Pakeha attitudes."

> Years ago, when Mani Bruce Mitchell was talking with the late Rangimārie Te Turuki Arikirangi Rose Pere, she told them Māori have always known about intersex people. "[Kaumātua] would say: 'this child has been sent to us to teach us something.' What a beautiful way of looking at and holding difference," Mitchell, who uses they/them pronouns and the honorific Mx, said.

"Which brings us to another Q." I continue. "Q stands for questioning, queer or sometimes a question mark is used. That leaves space for people who are still working out who they are. The longer listing adds on each grouping as it consolidates into an identifiable grouping of individuals who approach gender and identity from the same angle. It will be a good day when we can drop the list because we all accept everyone just as they are."

"That will be a long time coming," says Charity cynically.

"The good thing about the terminology list which Insideout produces is it gives you a glimpse into what the rainbow community itself thinks of the terms. It also gives you a look into the worldview of the community. For instance, there's a comment here." I flick back to the Insideout resource.

> LGBTQIA+ An acronym that stands for lesbian, gay, bisexual, transgender, queer, intersex, asexual, and more diverse sexualities, genders, and sex characteristics. It is used in a similar way to 'rainbow' but is often critiqued for centring Western understandings of gender, sex and sexuality.

"Once they start listening properly to the Other, the majority group finds there are myriad understandings out there which the Western/Pakeha/Palangi/Tauiwi/Cis mind has never thought or dreamed of and yet they are core to the Other's world view."

"We could make another set of letters – WPPTC – which I suppose is another way of expressing WASP, (white, anglo-saxon, protestant)," joked Charity.

"Or we could just meet each other as real people with a diverse way of looking at and dealing with life," I reply, suddenly weary and a little nauseous at how human beings keep on categorising other human beings into inadequate boxes.

"Indeed. Look at this term in that terminology list. It sums up the problems we're having in this area in both society and church."

> Heteronormativity: A framework of understanding sexuality that positions heterosexuality as the 'norm,' while marginalising all other sexualities or forms of non-heterosexual behaviour and inferring that they are 'abnormal.' This can look like assuming that people are straight/heterosexual, or othering people of different sexualities through such things as referring to 'the gay lifestyle.'[78]

I nod. "Just because a position is the minority numerically doesn't mean it is abnormal or wrong. It is simply different. Jesus said to everyone in the world, not only straight people; 'I am come that they might have life and have it more abundantly.'"

"Amen," says Charity. "Amen."

A thought occurs to me, and I continue.

"I guess it's the attitude that a minority must be wrong that led to the concept of conversion therapy. Churches and others have the fixed idea that heterosexuality is the norm, and more than that, is God-ordained as the only way to be. If you have a mindset that homosexuality is 'abnormal,' then you might want to help people to become 'normal.'"

Charity looks doubtful.

"From my experience of struggling with being different from the majority heterosexual position, I just can't see any way my 'gayness' could be removed from me, or that I could be changed into a straight person. It's not just whether I am sexually attracted to women, being gay has a much more pervasive influence through many different parts of my life. It's hard to explain."

I am interested in her reply, and it links in my mind with books I'd read some years ago.

"You've reminded me of the fantasy novels Philip Pullman wrote, where he depicted someone's 'soul' as a daemon, a small animal which accompanied the person wherever they went. In one novel of his trilogy, there were some evil characters who were kidnapping children and removing them from their daemon animals. The children got very weak and sick. Some died, that part of them was so much an integral factor in their life and wellbeing."

"That's right," exclaimed Charity, "I can't imagine a 'converted' gay person living a full and happy straight life."

"I was told of a couple of guys who are friends now, but one used to actually conduct conversion therapy and the other was the subject of his 'conversion' therapy. The first guy doesn't believe in CT anymore and is now helping and supporting the rainbow community. The other, who was the subject of the therapy, is now happily married to a man. I can't believe they are friends now. I would love to have been a fly on the wall during that conversation!"

While I was speaking, Charity has been putzing through her phone, "I'm looking up a definition of conversion therapy," she mutters. "Ah! Listen to this. This is Wikipedia's take on it."

> **Conversion therapy** is the pseudo-scientific practice of attempting to change an individual's sexual orientation from homosexual or bisexual to heterosexual using psychological, physical, or spiritual interventions. There is no reliable evidence that sexual orientation can be changed, and medical institutions warn that conversion therapy practices are ineffective and potentially harmful. Medical, scientific, and government organizations in the United States and the United Kingdom have expressed concern over the validity, efficacy and ethics of conversion therapy. Various jurisdictions around the world have passed laws against conversion therapy.
>
> The American Psychiatric Association (APA) opposes psychiatric treatment "based upon the assumption that homosexuality *per se* is a mental disorder or based upon the *a priori* assumption that a patient should change his/her sexual homosexual orientation"[9] and describes attempts to change a person's sexual orientation by practitioners as unethical.[6] The APA also states that the advancement of conversion therapy may cause social harm by disseminating unscientific views about sexual orientation.[10] In 2001, United States Surgeon General David Satcher issued a report stating that "there is no valid scientific evidence that sexual orientation can be changed."[15]
>
> Contemporary clinical techniques used in the United States have been limited to counselling, visualization, social skills training, psychoanalytic therapy, and spiritual interventions such as "prayer and group support and pressure,"[16] though there are some reports of aversive treatments through unlicensed practice as late as the early 2000s.

"That's a pretty authoritative dismissal of the idea from the APA. When the New Zealand government took a stance against it recently there were a record number of submissions received – 100,000. The petition which went to Parliament was signed by 160,000 and a TVNZ poll in September 2020 found 72% in favour of banning conversion therapy and only 14% opposed.[79] When the submissions were heard, there were different positions represented from different churches.[80] There's quite an interesting Radio New Zealand article about that. The debate on the first reading is also interesting reading.[81] It seems a few were being reactionary having decided that parental conversations might become outlawed – not true – or that question and answer sessions or pastoral encounters might become illegal – also not true. The select committee reported back to parliament in February 2022 after hearing all the submissions, and the Conversion Practices Prohibition Legislation Act 2022 became law later that month, with the support of all but eight MPs."[82]

"I think the most important part of this debate is that the discussion about it spreads the information that to attempt to 'convert' someone's sexual orientation is a dangerous and harmful thing to do, especially since it has no scientific evidence backing any kind of effectiveness," replied Charity. "How many countries in the world are introducing bans on conversion therapy?"

"Well," I replied, "further down in that Wikipedia article[83] there's a world map and a list of what is happening (or not) happening in 28 countries. In China there've been two cases where an individual who's been subjected to conversion therapy has been able to successfully sue but there is no nationwide ban. There is a terrible case described from South Africa in which three teens died as a result of 'conversion therapy.' In the US only some states have comprehensive bans in place. In Britain, the process of instituting a ban seems to have slowed down under a Conservative government. Other countries on the list are working on it. So there is quite a lot of work still to do around the world."

"That's not surprising, though hugely disappointing," replied Charity, "because there is still a lot of homophobia in the world."

"Indeed," I replied, feeling the familiar depression and nausea creeping over me.

"Well," said Charity, "I've got to go now, but I'm going to set myself the task of bringing something more optimistic to the table next week. Bye!"

"Bye," I echoed.

A quote came to mind "If you want to enjoy the rainbow, be prepared to endure the storm."[84] There were arguments and conflicts still to be engaged with on the way to equal acceptance of the various groups within the rainbow community. Storm was the right metaphor for the state of the weather we would encounter on the way.

12 – All are precious

[**CW**// Death through violence: p. 115.]

I find myself humming as I wait for Charity the next week. I notice my hum is an old Sunday School chorus learned from a very young age. I put words to the earworm which had been running through my head all morning.

> Jesus loves the little children, all the children of the world
> Red and yellow, black, and white, all are precious in his sight,
> Jesus loves the little children of the world.[85]

What naive words and what a simplistic, racist summary of ethnicity! Could it be adapted for our present conversation? What about…

> Jesus loves all human beings, all the people in the world
> Straight and lesbian and gay,
> Bi and trans and queer, all ways,
> Jesus loves all human beings in the world.

> Jesus loves all human beings, intersex, non-binary too
> Questioning, cis, butch and dyke
> all are precious in his sight
> Jesus loves all human beings in the world.

It wasn't going to make the Top 10, but at least it celebrated a range of rainbow orientations and identities. It was well known if ideas were attached to catchy tunes like this old marching song, those ideas became more accepted over time as people found themselves singing the lyrics. This old trick was used by writers of both Sunday school hymns and advertising jingles. Is Charity old enough to have been taught the original in Sunday school?

She is. I note it it's a trilby day today so she's in the zone. After our coffees appear, trim flat white for me, mocha for her, I explain my foray into chorus composition. We laugh and hum and try a few different arrangements of the words until Charity comments.

"It's strange you bring this up today. I was thinking through our conversations over the weeks. We've come up with some good information and discovered a lot of connections and misconnections. But, through it all, there's been the underlying feeling that the rainbow community are barely to be tolerated or at best need special accommodation in church or society. Remember how depressed we both felt at the end of last week when we were discussing conversion therapy? There's a subversive message that we rainbow types have to justify our presence and our lifestyle in a way heterosexuals do not. Straight people, it seems, are simply entitled to be here."

I nod. I notice that too.

Charity continues. "I said I'd come with something more optimistic this time. I've researched notable gay people and their accomplishments. Just to show, you know, that homosexual people with their 'out-of-the-norm' identities function well in this world. They, along with those entitled straights, contribute an enormous amount to our health and well-being, to enjoyment and pleasure but also to substantive issues in politics and education. It kind of fits with these lyrics highlighting and valuing everyone."

"Sounds good," I reply. "Whom have you discovered?"

"First, on an international Wikipedia list I used for a quick survey there are 56 New Zealanders who are notable and either gay, lesbian or bisexual."[86]

She continues, checking her notes. "The list contains 17 sportspeople. Among them are several female sporting notables including three cricketers, four footballers, two Olympic rugby players, and one Olympic rower along with two other rugby union players. There is also a woman hockey player and a female road racing cyclist. The list also includes male sportspeople, though not as many. There's a male Olympic equestrian and a male short track speed skater too."

Charity keeps talking. She is on a roll. "We can't make that into any kind of percentage because who knows the total number of sportspeople in different disciplines in New Zealand, but it seems a good number to me. Male rugby players of course keep their sexual orientation on the down low if they are at all rainbow, but I wouldn't be surprised if there are gay members of the All Blacks now and in the past. The article made it plain they include only people definitely out and not people only rumoured to be so."

"Do New Zealand rainbow community people appear in other categories?"

"There are quite a few politicians," replies Charity. "New Zealand's current deputy prime minister is gay, and 11 politicians are listed in total. That includes gay members of parliament with more right-wing political preferences. Dame Marilyn Waring was a significant National politician in the late 1970s, early 1980s and is still a respected academic in economics."

"This is interesting, all these sportspeople and politicians," I comment. "The stereotype of gay people is that they are prominent in the arts."

"There are those kinds of occupations represented on the list too," replies Charity. "If you include chefs as being in the arts, the total comes to 16. Two chefs in fact, five writers, two involved with dance, two actors and seven who are well known in the music field in different ways."

"There's one really sad entry," adds Charity. "Jeff Whittington is simply listed as 'murder victim.' He was killed in 1999 when he was only 14 years old. I followed the footnote to a newspaper article. Listen to this: 'Jeff Whittington, age 14 and effeminate, seems to have paid a high price for his nail polish and purple hair; in May he was beaten and stomped to death, allegedly by two men in their twenties who believed him to be gay.'[87] From the article it seemed like he and the boys who killed him were all much the worse for drink and/or drugs, and they didn't mean to kill him they said, but the attack sounds vicious."

"That's over two decades ago, but something similar could still happen in New Zealand given the right – or wrong – circumstances," I comment. "The defence of provocation in murder cases was removed from New Zealand law in 2009, but one thesis written in 2013 argues that lighter sentences are still given for murder in response to unwanted homosexual advances."

I tap and swipe my tablet screen and bring up the abstract of the thesis.

This paper discusses sentencing in New Zealand homicide cases in which the offence was prompted by a homosexual advance in light of the abolition of the partial defence of provocation.

The author argues that, despite the concerns around sentencing in homosexual advance cases that partly led to the abolition of the partial defence, there has been no real change in the way these cases are being sentenced. This paper suggests that prejudice against homosexuals may be a significant contributing factor toward the low sentences that have continued to be given to offenders in unwanted homosexual advance cases.[88]

Charity nods sadly. "That just goes to show that being openly out in New Zealand society may still carry quite a lot of risk."

I nod in my turn. Gay, lesbian, and bisexual people who are open about their orientation, especially when they lead public lives, are admirable. I take up the conversation.

"Recent laws making civil unions and then same sex marriage legal have largely been due to support of gay politicians."

"Though there were also some famous heterosexual allies who came to the party too!" adds Charity and we laugh. Right wing politician Maurice Williamson had spoken in the debate about messages sent to him on the same sex marriage bill. He'd said in his speech: 'One of the messages that I had was that this bill was the cause of our drought. Well, in the Pakuranga electorate this morning, it was pouring with rain. We had the most enormous, big gay rainbow across my electorate.' It was one of those political moments which 'went viral.'

Charity continues as we sober up. "Out of the gay politicians, Lousia Wall could have been in both the sporting and politician lists. She was a member of the Silver Ferns national netball team, and also was part of the national women's rugby team that won the first World Cup. She was New Zealand Woman Rugby Player of the Year in 1997."

"That's right. In 2012, it was Louisa who entered the bill redefining marriage to include same sex marriage into the draw of private member's bills, which are then considered by parliament. It was introduced to Parliament in July of that year and passed into law the following year in April 2013."

"That made New Zealand the 13th nation in the world to allow same sex marriage," adds Charity. "That's not bad, not bad at all. It has a big flow-on effect beyond couples' personal lives. It was cool when Emma Twigg won her Olympic gold medal in 2021 that the reporters in New Zealand interviewed her wife, who hadn't been able to be in Tokyo too because of the covid pandemic. It made Emma's orientation very public, but I didn't hear or see any adverse comments about that."

I agree. "There was a cool piece in an article about Louisa and the passing of the bill. She likened it to Treaty of Waitangi settlement acts passed by Parliament and added that 'the passing of the Bill was like winning a 'World Cup final.' There was a crowd in the gallery and they sang a waiata when the bill was passed. I was in England on study leave at the time and it was in all the UK press and TV news. I was so proud of New Zealand and to be a New Zealander."

My mind jumps elsewhere. "Was Tabby Besley on that list?"

"No, should she have been?"

"I'd say so! Tabby runs the charity InsideOut and won a Queen's young leader's award in 2015. I remember it well because she coloured her hair purple in honour of the occasion when she received her award from the Queen at Buckingham Palace. (I wonder what the Queen made of that!). Tabby's a great advocate for the LGBTQI community."

"And I noticed Michael Parmenter isn't included. He's definitely 'out' publicly. His choreography has graphically portrayed some of his struggles. He's famous for *A Long Undressing*, and I loved his *Jerusalem the Dance Opera*. Look what it says here about him." I'd been looking Michael up on my tablet and I turn the screen towards Charity.

> And I remember Parmenter telling his life story, the boy from Southland, born in the 1950s, gay in a conservative Christian family, how he got from there to dance, and then to a show based not on choreography but on words, although there was some very lovely dance in it too. That was *A Long Undressing*.
>
> So many times, Parmenter has broken with expectation. He is an artist on the edge, inviting us with each new work to travel with him somewhere new, to thrill to the aesthetic splendour and to what the work tells us, or asks us, about what it means to live in this time and in this place.[89]

I suggest another coffee is in order and go to the counter. I leave Charity looking through the lists she'd researched. When I return, having ordered my caramel latte and her Americano, she slants her tablet so I can see the screen.

"I found other lists too, one for transgender people and one for intersex members of the rainbow community. I found Mani Bruce Mitchell on the intersex list. They're the only New Zealander on that list. It is good that Mani is so visible and their Queen's Birthday honour will have helped with that. Yes, they state in this interview here that they felt a little uncomfortable accepting the Honour because of the baggage around such an establishment thing, but then they realised it was giving great visibility to the intersex community, so they were thrilled about that aspect of it."[90]

"I'm not surprised there is only one person listed for New Zealand," she continues. "Look how short this list is too compared to the other. It is not a life position which is easy to be public about. But see here, here's an Australian, Morgan Carpenter. He designed the intersex flag with its purple circle and yellow background. See the comment he makes about the symbolism of the flag."

> The flag is comprised of a golden yellow field, with a purple circle emblem. The colours and circle don't just avoid referencing gender stereotypes, like the colours pink and blue, they seek to completely avoid use of symbols that have anything to do with gender at all. Instead, the circle is unbroken and unornamented, symbolising wholeness and completeness, and our potentialities. We are still fighting for bodily autonomy and genital integrity, and this symbolises the right to be who and how we want to be.[91]

"Mani brought purple and yellow colours into an event we were running," I comment. "It was an education to me at the time that the intersex community had their own colours. See Morgan's comment that they've avoided the usual pink and blue."

Charity nods as I speak. "The trans colours use pink, blue and white, don't they? The international list of notable trans people has five New Zealanders. Politician Georgina Beyer (1957-), weightlifter Laurel Hubbard (1978-), the entertainer and activist Carmen Rupe (1936-2011) who's listed as New Zealand/Australian, television presenter Ramon Te Wake (1976-) and Eliana Rubashkyn (1988-) who's listed as New Zealand/Columbian. She has an interesting note beside her name. She's a pharmacist, former refugee and the first transgender woman recognised as a woman under International Law and the UNHCR. The UN did that because Eliana got trapped in Hong Kong where she was threatened with deportation. Eliana's story of that time is harrowing reading."[92]

"How harrowing too is Laurel Hubbard's life at the moment!" I exclaim. "She was accepted into the Olympic women's weightlifting under conditions about testosterone levels, but she was at the epicentre of a media circus at the 2020 Games in Tokyo (held in 2021). In the end, she totally failed at the lifting at the Olympics. How much of that was due to the scrutiny which she felt? People tend to think anyone trans or queer are exhibitionists, but Laurel is shy. It must be very difficult."

"I am sure it is," responded Charity. "Georgina Beyer, who we've already spoken about, is one transwoman who outwardly always seems very calm. She's got such an air of gravitas and dignity and is always superbly groomed. Her political career's interesting. She entered Parliament in 2000 after having been the mayor of Carterton for five years, the world's first transgender mayor."

"She then served in Parliament for seven years, this time becoming the world's first transgender Member of Parliament. Georgina often faced intrusive questions. Look at this piece here."

> In a December 2002 interview, Beyer said: "I get asked questions no other politician would ever have to answer. Regarding the surgery, you know. 'Did it hurt?' or 'When you have sex now as a woman, is it different to how you had sex as a man?' Well, honey, obviously."[93]

"And here too."

> In her speech to Parliament on the Prostitution Reform Act 2003, Beyer identified herself as a former sex worker. She is credited with influencing three MPs to vote for the Bill, which passed with 60 votes for, 59 against with one abstention.

"And this piece is from her maiden speech."

> Mr. Speaker, I can't help but mention the number of firsts that are in this Parliament. Our first Rastafarian [*Nándor Tánczos*]… our first Polynesian woman [*Luamanuvao Winnie Laban*]… and yes, I have to say it, I guess, I am the first transsexual in New Zealand to be standing in this House of Parliament. This is a first not only in New Zealand, ladies and gentlemen, but also in the world. This is an historic moment. We need to acknowledge that this country of ours leads the way in so many

aspects. We have led the way for women getting the vote. We have led the way in the past, and I hope we will do so again in the future in social policy and certainly in human rights.

"She's been a great role model," I agree, "but, you know, she let people know in recent times that she had to go on welfare at one stage. Sometimes a person is famous and speaks publicly but doesn't always have a good steady income to back that up. When people who've been honoured in the Queen's Honours for example, speak publicly are they are being paid for the speaking they do? Can they afford to be such figureheads?"

"I hadn't thought of that," responds Charity, her face thoughtful. "I guess that's right. That also applies to singers and actors who were once famous but no longer. It would depend on how much money they'd been able to invest when times were good."

"Were there any other lists on Wikipedia which are on our topic?" I ask, to keep away the somewhat depressed feeling which was creeping over me. I am very impressed by what the rainbow community do in society as individuals, but many of their stories still seem to have their dark side of prejudice and neglect, abuse, disadvantage, and mistreatment.

"There's a non-binary queer listing," says Charity, returning to her table screen. "Two 'part-New Zealanders' are on that list. First, Richard O'Brien listed as a British New Zealander who's named as a writer, actor, TV presenter, and theatre performer. The birth date given is 1942. Richard's notable as the author of the *Rocky Horror Show* – which has a near-cult following in the States. I didn't know a New Zealander had written that! Richard's come out as transgender relatively recently and estimates being about 70% male and 30% female, saying it is easier being different in the arts compared with, say, primary school teaching."[94]

"The second on the list simply has 'twentieth century' as a birthdate. A.W. Peet is named as a New Zealander Canadian physicist who deals in string theory and quantum gravity. There's a couple of contrasts in lifestyles and interests, *Rocky Horror* and String Theory!"

"I think I remember something about A.W. Peet's reaction to Jordan Peterson's[95] refusal to use 'they' as a pronoun when others request it. Peterson released a YouTube piece on the issue of how a proposed bill on hate speech might interfere with freedom of speech. He's generally dismissive of political correctness. It was about five years ago. Let me see if I can find the article. Here it is," I push the tablet round to where Charity can see the screen.[96]

> A. W. Peet, a physics professor who identifies as non-binary and uses the pronoun 'they,' expressed disappointment with Peterson's comments.

> "It doesn't really matter whether he thinks we exist or not because we do. I just wanted to say, 'Excuse me, I exist. I'm non-binary and I'm also a full professor with the University of Toronto with tenure," said Peet. "So this is me standing up saying I don't think this is good enough."

"It is interesting isn't it, these two people, Richard and A.W., dealing with the same unease in society about non-binary and transgender positions, but in different ways in their own arenas of life. One writes a risqué musical and the other speaks out in public – both must have required courage."

"Yes," agrees Charity. "I see Peet mentions being tenured. It would be difficult for someone not tenured in the North American academic system to speak out like that. It's still brave of him to go public."

"True. What lesbian women have been role models during your development, Charity?"

I'm curious to know who has been specifically important in her life.

Charity's face lights up and she jumps right in. "Billy Jean King and Martina Navratilova were my heroines when I was playing tennis at school. Did you know I played for the school team in my last two years at high school? I did admire Billy Jean King's fight for equality for women tennis players. Remember she played a man to show that a woman could beat a man in a game? Both those women were early sporting role models of mine. Now more women are playing other 'masculine' kinds of sports." She does air quotes around the M word. "We see them on those lists as footballers and rugby union players, for example."

I probe further. "Who's been important for you in music?"

"In music, I'm a bit retro. I love Dusty Springfield's music, it's so strong and vibrant. And I love K D Laing's stuff. Because of my Mum's taste in music, I'd always liked the music of both Joan Armatrading and Janis Ian, so it was a bonus when I heard they'd entered partnerships with women in the 2000s."

"Then in New Zealand of course, now there are Lynda and Jools Topp and Anika Moa. It's significant that contemporary musicians are more open about their orientation. Other singers from decades ago seem to have kept their orientation quiet, but when the opportunity for civil partnerships or same sex marriage came through, they've taken them up. The existence of the legal possibility of such partnerships suggests there's wider acceptance in society, though that depends where in the world you live."

I break in. "A lot of contemporary music relies on couple imagery which most people assume is male/female. It may have been urged on them by record producers to keep quiet about their orientation in case it affected their 'brand.' Any favourites in the writing and acting fields?"

"Never warmed to Katherine Mansfield's writing at school when we had to study it, though that's not something you can say to a lot of people in New Zealand. I remember my mother being keen on Alice Walker's writing, especially *The Colour Purple*.[97] Audre Lorde[98] and Mary Oliver[99] are two poets my mother introduced me to as well. As a teenager, Paula Boock's *Dare Truth or Promise*[100] was very significant for my coming out later. It was the first time I'd read a young adults' book with a heroine who was like me.

"Actors? I liked the movie Julianne Moore and Annette Bening did about a gay couple, though as real people they are straight as far as I know. My mother again was very keen on *The West Wing* TV series and keeps watching reruns. I've picked up the habit. I was thrilled to find out Lily Tomlin, the actor who's that quirky secretary to the President is a lesbian. I thought she had real pizazz in that part. I've seen her in other films and TV series and the same energy comes through."

She carries on reminiscing. "Ellen de Generes' been interesting because before her talkback show, her sitcom *Ellen* dealt with some big LGBT issues. I've watched some old episodes. I remember being told about the fuss over Anne Heche's orientation relating to acting parts after she and Ellen were an item. Of course, Ellen's married now to another actor, Portia di Rossi."

"What about politicians? Anyone strike a chord with you?"

How many role models can contemporary young lesbian women find.

"Oh, what about the prime ministers of Iceland and Serbia who are both gay women? Imagine a country where that can happen! Especially in Serbia it wouldn't have been obvious to me that might have happened. Of course, we've said that New Zealand has a gay (male) deputy prime minister and when that finally happened there was very little comment. I also love the stories of how Maryan Street and Marilyn Waring wielded great influence in their time in the New Zealand Parliament. Chloe Swarbrick and Jan Logie are contemporary lesbian MPs who impress me."

Charity thinks for a moment more and then adds. "There are a lot of prominent women whom I admire, and am influenced by. When I know they are lesbian as well, that gives it an extra edge, though. Being able to see women like me, with the same orientation, doing well and making a distinctive contribution, helps me feel more entitled to be here. It helps me feel I can do great things too because they have already done great things, no matter what the odds. Some of their autobiographies and biographies certainly show it hasn't been easy. It would be good to be able to look around the church and see women who are openly gay in positions of leadership."

I nod. "I guess there are many lesbian women doing great jobs all through society. It's writers, actors, politicians, and sportspeople who get publicity and, in the process, get sometimes unwelcome scrutiny of their personal lives. We know they are lesbian because it becomes a matter of public record for good or for ill."

After another moment thinking, I speak carefully. "It is great they encourage you. Just taking a step back, however, how annoying it is that we must state or need to know what orientation a person is! That is their private business. I don't get asked if I am straight, though I do get asked if I have children (being childless is another unusual life position for a married straight woman). People are people, whatever their orientation. We are all equally human. We don't need brilliant lesbian politicians or sportswomen who excel to prove anything about the worth of lesbians as a group in society."

"Thank you! It's good to hear that!"

Following up an idea which had just popped into my head, I scroll through my phone. "When you know Janis Ian is gay, her 1975 song *At Seventeen* takes on another dimension. Look at the lyrics. It's a haunting melody, but when you look at the lyrics with new eyes, knowing she is gay, they seem to me they contain a truth which she probably had to hide from the general public back then. She names the problem as her not being clear-skinned blonde and beautiful. Maybe it was more than that."[101]

We listen to the song to its end, sharing Charity's ear buds. Do seventeen-year-old girls still feel like ugly ducklings now because they are gay in a homophobic society? My heart aches for them. In 1974, did Janis Ian really think she was ugly because that male/female attraction wasn't happening for her? Who decides who is ugly? Since when were teenage heterosexual males the arbiters of beauty?

Charity says she has to go, and after arranging our next meeting, she leaves, ear buds in place, listening again to Janis as she swings down the street.

After she leaves, I get a herbal tea and sit and reflect on the mature Janis I'd stumbled across on YouTube when I was finding her 'Seventeen' song.

A few years ago, after she had married her lover in a same sex ceremony in Canada, Janis presented a wry look at how the two women negotiated attitudes, dress codes, language, and titles. The reality, she says, in her funny yet poignant monologue, is that though they are now married, only in some states of the USA is their union legally recognised. Her introduction and comedic song on the topic are presented with a mixture of wry humour and profound truth, 'Love has no colour and heart has no sex,' she sings in her song *Married in London*. Underlying pain, however, can be discerned beneath the surface.[102]

This song reminded me that just as the civil rights legislation in the US had not automatically and immediately made life alright for black people, same sex marriage legislation, while ground-breaking, could not do the whole job of creating worldwide acceptance for members of the rainbow community.

It is easier, perhaps, to read novels where characters can be emphatic without fear of pursed lips or weird reactions in the audience visible in front of you. Take the forthright opinion, expressed by Alice Walker when she talks about how *The Color Purple* came to her.

> I am an expression of the divine, just like a peach is, or a fish is. I have a right to be this way. ... I can't apologise for that, nor can I change it, nor do I want to.[103]

13 – All are equally on the journey to being fully human

Charity looks up as I enter *The Cup* and waves me over. Under the black beanie, pulled down over her red curls, she looks mischievous.

"What's up?" I ask, thinking I needed a coffee quickly after the frustrating admin meeting I'd just attended.

"Don't worry," says Charity correctly interpreting my look. "I've ordered us both a vanilla latte."

"Phew!" I brushed my hand over my brow in exaggerated relief. "So, what's with the mysterious look?"

"I found this!" She waves a slim volume in front of me. I catch the familiar picture of a winding path and the title *Wherever you are, You are on the Journey* on the cover.[104]

"You didn't tell me you'd written this! It's fascinating. I thought as I read the first few chapters, that the path from one faith stage to another must be like the path a straight person needs to take to fully understand the significance of the rainbow position."

"Mmm, you might be right. All developmental paths have their stages of deepening understanding. I hadn't connected the two before."

"Who's Guy?"

"Who's Guy? Oh. The story in Chapter 1? A few people have asked me that and wondered why he didn't appear again in the book. Guy was a member at our church about five years ago, before you joined us. His partner Daniel didn't come often, mainly just for special occasions and when Guy was doing something in the service."

"It says here that Guy had found his dissatisfaction with church growing the more he came out," comments Charity.

"Yes, I was sad about that. I didn't think it had to be like that, but it was at the height of the nastiest parts of the gay debate in the church and the previous senior minister wasn't 'out' about being pro-gay in those days. Guy felt he couldn't be completely himself around church."

"Why is it so difficult for members of the rainbow community to integrate with church even when the 'gay thing' isn't being discussed? Are we rainbow types not capable of a spiritual journey like straight people?" asks Charity, her brow furrowing as she ponders my answer.

"Of course, they, you, are capable of journeying spiritually. In fact, your discoveries about yourself as a gay person are an integral part of that journey. Spirituality and sexuality are closely intertwined. They're both parts of ourselves which have roots into the very deepest part of our psyche or soul. That's why unfortunately, when religious leaders aren't aware of that close intertwining, they can mistake spiritual happenings for sexual ones and vice versa, leading to harassment and abuse. People can be so unaware of that."

I continue quickly.

"I think there are at least four aspects to the issue of spiritual journeys and sexuality."

"One is a person's orientation. Not under their control. Whether or not it is nature or nurture or a mixture of both, a gay person is what they are. Same is true for straight or bisexual individuals. In some ways spiritually, a gay person and a straight person are the same in this regard. They're both surrounded by Love every moment of every day. A few years ago, I would have described us all as God's loved children, but I've been trying not to use personalised God language quite so much."

Charity nods. "I got that from *Wherever you are...*"

"Then there's what the church community experience is like if you're in a relationship or not. That influences the church experience and spiritual journeys for both straight and gay people. Singles can sometimes find fitting into a church community difficult if most of the members are couples. I know I've found occasionally that, not having had children, I don't fit well into all church activities. It's been a problem with gay people in relationships because of this conservative morality standard which has been argued. Then too, even in a gay-friendly church, the visuals used are mostly heterosexual. Often there are not enough words which 'belong' to the gay community being used, or the illustrations and jokes are all about couples – that's hard for straight singles as well. The whole experience is often not diverse enough."

"A third issue is that, even if there aren't any community issues with relationships, it can be hard to journey spiritually when you are linked with another person intimately. They may or may not be on the same wavelength. That might require some negotiation about whether it's the coffeeshop on Sunday morning or the church pew."

Charity grins. Sometimes Katy got annoyed about how much Charity was involved with church and Charity would take a weekend off church to do things with her on Sundays.

"And the fourth?" she prompts.

"The fourth thing I'd want to say, perhaps the most important, is that there's how an individual wants to journey – or perhaps what stage they are at. I meant that book title, *Wherever you are, You are on the Journey.* You can be years down the track like I am, or just starting out. Sometimes you're standing still, but your feet are still on the path. You might have wandered away from home like the prodigal son, but you're still journeying."

I thought for a moment then continued.

"Gay, lesbian and bisexual children might be brought up, as I was, in a fundamentalist church. That's hard because they will run up against all those negative attitudes, but they still might love the other theology they've learned there and the worship style they've been socialised in, singing contemporary music with a band. They might like their theology to be black and white and reasonably straightforward (if you will excuse the pun)."

"Then there are rainbow people who, just like some heteros do, want to question and wrestle with theological ideas – not only with the theology of sexual orientation. If that's the route which calls you, you'll find yourself in a very small group. The rainbow community is a small percentage of the general population, a smaller percentage of them go to church and a smaller percentage still want to go through the disenchantment process and on beyond it to be re-enchanted with the spiritual journey again, as I described in *Wherever you are...*"

Charity is nodding thoughtfully and comments, "Anyone who's come out to friends and family and church may have an advantage in the questioning faith stage. I found the coming out process required a lot of soul searching, a lot of becoming more and more self-aware both of my orientation and my own attitude to that. I also found I had to be more aware of what others' reactions meant. When someone gasps at you saying you're gay – it may mean they're shocked, but they may simply be surprised and processing what you've just said. The more aware I became about it all, the more I could allow for different meanings behind another's behaviours and words."

I nodded in my turn and added, "Deepening the spiritual journey, answering what Jung called the invitation to the second journey, is hard enough. It's even harder when you're making that crucial journey out of the closet at the same time, even if internally you can gain strength from both. That's what I was sorry Guy couldn't see. He felt great joy and freedom coming out and being open about his relationship with Daniel. I also hoped it could be replicated in the joy and freedom of a new way of journeying spiritually too."

"Did you know, I helped Guy and Daniel to do a relationship blessing they wanted? It was well before civil unions and same sex marriage. They wanted to hold a ceremony where they made it clear to friends and family they were together. They chose a gorgeous place, we ordered an arch of rainbow balloons and it was Guy who sewed two sets of thin stoles in each colour from the rainbow. That formed the framework for their vows to each other. Each 'stole' represented a quality they loved in the other. They took turns putting a stole around the other's neck and telling him about the quality they loved in him. It was so sincere and beautiful, much better than many hetero weddings I have attended. It was spiritual in the best sense of the word. It was a great pity that sense of spirituality was not welcomed then in our church or that Guy could not take the risk (a big one, I know!) of bringing that spirituality to church with him."

Charity eyes are starry. I wonder if she is taking notes for a ceremony of her own.

"That sounds so cool. I've kept my orientation and my spiritual walk separate. Perhaps, it's because there are few stories in the Bible that reflect my life."

"There are a lot more relevant stories than people think," I said. "There's David and Jonathan, for example. Read that story through in the end of the first book of Samuel and the beginning of the second book of Samuel. Even the 'funny old Bible' states that Jonathan loved

David as himself and that the bond between them was immediate. Love at first sight? Jonathan later takes a huge risk to warn David of his father's anger. Even after he is killed, when David finds out Jonathan's son is still alive, he immediately searches the boy out and takes care of him in his own household."[105] There's a very strong devotion between the two men.

"Then there's a similar bond between Naomi and her daughter in law Ruth – they wouldn't have been lovers, but they were two women in their own household who had to fend for themselves in a patriarchal society. What Ruth says to Naomi en route to Bethlehem is often used at weddings as a vow from one hetero partner to the other, so why not from one woman to her wife? I'd love to hear it used from one partner to the other in a same sex marriage ceremony."

> "Where you go I will go, and where you stay I will stay. Your people will be my people and your God my God. Where you die I will die, and there I will be buried. May the LORD deal with me, be it ever so severely, if even death separates you and me."[106]

"There's also the very strong sisterly bond between Mary and Martha – again they are sisters, not lesbian lovers, but there's another two-woman relationship which has typical tensions and jealousies within it."

Charity is looking interested and now says quietly, "and we've said before that Jesus mixed with all sorts of people, didn't he? As far as we know he never married. I know people joke that he lived with his mother and got around with a bunch of blokes, but it does mean that we can see him just as he was, not as a father or a husband, just as an individual. He seemed to have had a lot of different kinds of relationships with diverse people."

I nod in agreement. "Also, because of his adventuresome theology, the church of his time, the synagogue and its rabbis, found him a bit of a handful to deal with. It suggests he might understand what rainbow people go through when they are being faithful to their call to be followers of him as well as true to their orientation," I pointed out.

Charity looked interested in that idea. "So we might have some advantages in understanding Jesus' words. We might understand from personal experience what it means to be marginalised. That's an advantage in working with others who are different and need support and friendship. Those, in fact, whom Jesus seemed to like to spend his precious time with."

"Yes, the process of coming out, painful as it can be, gives you understandings and skills which are valuable in the spiritual journey – letting go, being brave, getting acquainted with your inner thoughts, being prepared to see what is inside yourself which you hadn't noticed, or allowed yourself to notice before."

I thought for a minute, then continued. "You'll see, if you read on in *Wherever you are…*, that I see the spiritual journey as a quest. It's a quest to find out how to be fully human. A straight person can do that, so can a lesbian, a gay man or a bisexual person. Non-binaries definitely are discovering what it means for them to be human. It applies equally as a quest for those born intersex. And wouldn't you say that the transition process for a transgendered person is a real journey into their very Self?"

Charity nodded. I can tell she is thinking hard as I talk.

"I remember Dave Tomlinson saying in a *Holy Shed* YouTube video once 'God is at the end of every road.'[107] It's a different way of saying 'Wherever you are, you are on the journey.' Your journey might be shaped differently, but it is still that quest for you to find out what it means for you to be fully human. Your answer to that will be different from my answer for me, but we will both equally be in God while we travel there."

I added: "Someone said once something like as we grow closer to being fully human, we approach the divine. Not that we become divine, but that being fully human is a divine thing to be. That's why Jesus was such a powerful force in his world and now in ours. He of all people seemed to have achieved a full authentic humanity. And we say, don't we, that we see God most fully through him? Being human and being divine, instead of being opposites, are much closer than we thought."

Charity is engrossed. She opens and closes her mouth, choosing her words as she takes a while to speak.

"That's what I've loved about these discussions we've been having. You've reminded me of things like, I was baptised before the church knew I was gay, and grace was shown to me as a tiny baby just like everyone else. That can't be taken away from me."

"Each Pride month you've given reflections in church that remind me I am 'allowed' to be here, just like anyone else. In those reflections too, you've burst some of the arguments against that – as we've done here."[108]

"You've reminded me that Love surrounds me every moment of every day. Again, just like everyone else."

"You've directed me to Alice Walker talking about *The Color Purple* (and I loved it so much I learned it off by heart):

> I am an expression of the divine, just like a peach is, or a fish is. I have a right to be this way. I can't apologise for that, nor can I change it, nor do I want to.[109]

"It made me get the book and read it. I found that wonderful chapter where the name of the book is used, and the chapter is all about what God is like and what God is not like. It made me wonder if the whole book was actually about God in a very profoundly different way. I also memorised this bit. She looked at me, a slight flush rising on her cheeks and quoted:

> "…when it happen, you can't miss it. It sort of like you know what, she say, grinning and rubbing high up on my thigh. Shug! I say.
>
> Oh, she say, God love all them feelings. That's some of the best stuff God did. And when you know God loves 'em you enjoys 'em a lot more. You can just relax, go with everything that's going, and praise God by liking what you like.
>
> God don't think it dirty? I ast.
>
> Naw, she say God made it."[110]

"With all of this, the discussion, the books, the research, I've become more and more sure that I am the right person in the right body with the right orientation for me. I've become more and more sure that I am on a spiritual journey wherever I am. I've become more and more sure that I belong in the church as much as anyone else. I'm even more sure than I already was that I am loved – by Jesus, by God, the Spirit – and actually by a lot of Christians, only not some."

I smiled, gladdened by her passionate certainty. I think of something I heard years ago in a Pride service when I was a ministry student.

"There's a poem which expresses some of that. It's called *Saxophone Spirit* by the famous poet 'Anon'. It really needs to be read over a Jan Gabarek saxophone solo.[111] I'll email it to you,[112] so you can read it with the music, but here's a bit of it." I tapped and scrolled and brought up the script.

Where are you God?

Are you
in the brief split second's hesitation
before the heart-catching moment
when the sax starts its sensual swirling sweep of sound
tingling down through her body
right from her cranium
to finally reach her toes.

Was that moment of singing silence
that possession of singing sound
…you?

Where are you God?

Are you in the brief split second's hesitation
before the heart-catching moment
when she trusts the gay woman in front of her
with her secret
that she too, is queer?
and the woman smiles
for she already knows.

Where are you, God?

will there even be a brief, split second's hesitation
before you smile too
before she senses your joy filled presence
before in a heart catching moment
she knows
you are
that you are for her
what the church cannot be.

"You see," I said, "though it would be lovely, totally fantastic to be fully accepted by the church, that's not what is ultimately important.

It is the integration of you as human being with Love, with light, with spirit which is the end goal. And that is so possible. It is so vital for your deepest wellbeing. I can see it already happening in you."

Charity eyes were bright with unshed tears.

"And at the end the poem finishes:"

> the saxophone breathes into her soul,
> blowing where it chooses.
> She hears the sound of it,
>
> but does not know from whence it comes
> or whither it goes.
>
> You are here God….
> wind of love…
> saxophone Spirit….
> birthing from above!

We sit together in silence, the hiss and bustle of the café falling away as we savour the moment, a heart catching moment when we sense Love surrounding us in this intersection of time and space with the Other.

14 – Into 'the future where meaning may be found'[113]

I stretch luxuriously in the sun. I love study leave with its opportunities to stretch the brain, open the heart, and rest the body. Fragrance from nearby lavender wafts past, mixing with roses' scent from the path beyond and the aroma of coffee rises from my rainbow-striped cup. Bees quietly buzz their busy way from flower to flower. They remind me of myself when in full harness. A little too busy all the time.

I am content in this quiet space. Feeling even more content because of the email that morning.

It's a while since Charity and I had talked face to face. She'd entered honours and is working on her dissertation which she's based on one of the US studies we'd discussed. She's replicating their research on the effect of religious connection on suicide rates in young people, comparing experiences of straight and gay adolescents in New Zealand. Already she'd found that in more secular New Zealand, young people participate less in religion than their North American counterparts. Would that change the overall results? She's keen to find out. So am I.

Charity writes she is in the throes of finishing up her project. There is academic interest in her work. She's been offered a scholarship which comprises an internship with a national organisation specialising in mental health. The deal is that she trains on the job to be a psychotherapist. They are open to her desire to specialise in working with rainbow young people.

"I want to make a difference in my own community," she writes. "It's vital rainbow youth get good access to mental health resources and are prioritised with help tailored to their specific context. Remember that study you found where therapists claimed they treated gay clients the same as other clients, but their delivery of services was biased? I don't want that to happen here."

I pick up her email from the coffee table beside me. It's a delight to read again the ways different elements we'd touched on over the past few months were now helping Charity to find her vocation. I read on.

"It was an important week," she continues, "when we discovered simultaneously the misunderstandings because of poor translations. Surely evangelicals who value following the Bible would want to adjust their attitudes when it is shown that the long-term loving relationships of gay Christians, who want to be in leadership, is definitely not what is being disallowed in the scriptures. I would expect them to be consistent enough to admit that the biblical interpretation has not been careful enough."

"Another landmark for me was our discussion about the quality of a relationship being more important, for all relationships, than the gender of the partners in the relationship. It seemed to me that both gay and straight Christians need that reminder."

She goes back to describing her own future hopes and dreams.

"I particularly hope we can attract young people struggling with the taboos laid on them by fundamentalist and conservative religion. The organisation I'll be interning with has church people on their board who are keen to run educational programmes alongside their counselling services. That Bible stuff we talked about will come in handy. I'll include too Haidt's listing of the different values used at either end of the spectrum. I'm so excited. What I learned from our conversations can spread wider. I can focus on those who need to hear they are OK just as they are."

I'm excited just reading her words. As a minister I'm uncomfortably aware I mostly interact with churched people. Administration soaks up time and energy. And, I know, many leave the church because of its draconian attitude towards the rainbow community. Now even more don't come to church at all. The 'Nones' are the increasing number of people who tick "No Religion" in census forms. In the 2013 census they outnumbered the Christian population in New Zealand for the first time.[114]

I read on to the next part of Charity's email. Katy and she are planning to get married when they finish their dissertations, probably next year. Charity writes they'll get in touch about whether I'd be able to marry them and if so, where. I grin, a sappy smile spreading over my face. Same sex marriages are such fun. I make a mental note to remind Charity, however, to check out the Janis Ian talk/song on getting married.[115] The poignancy of Janis' retelling of her experiences in negotiating other's reactions, the choosing of appropriate clothing for the ceremony and her own unease at the unfamiliar, was a compassionate cautionary tale for gay people involved in same sex unions. I also see same sex wives and husbands making various arrangements in having children. It made me think of the baby naming ceremony I'd led years ago for two lesbian friends and their baby son.[116] Everything is different when you don't fit the majority position. Yet, if you don't have a gathering at that point, you miss out on the solidarity of friends and the chance to thank people for their help and support.

I skim down the email further. I feel again the surprise, pleasure, then thankfulness I'd felt reading Charity's decision that she will hang in with the church a bit longer. The church doesn't know how much it needs people like her to stay, even if it doesn't always appreciate their presence.

She writes, "I learned so much from our conversations and the reading you encouraged me to do. Some of us need to hang in there. Let's not leave the church only to the conservatives. I'm hoping to get in touch with youth leaders in other parishes and see if we can create an educational programme about the bible stuff you and I discussed. Maybe we could get a synergy going between my new workplace and local churches. Work could provide teaching personnel and resources, and churches provide the audiences. Getting people reading David Gushee would be enough of an achievement alone!"

Her email sweeps on. "No offence, my oldie friend, but my generation needs to be spearheading this work into the future. There's something about hearing this stuff from someone who is not only gay like you but also young like you. I've learned heaps from you about the framework within which this debate lies which will always inform my praxis, but the whole rainbow scene's changed in the last couple of decades and continues to change. As we learned from Skye!"

I imagine the emerald twinkle in Charity's eyes as she wrote that last sentence. Skye's non-binary coming out broadsided many, including her cousin. Skye is a good ally for Charity's project of meeting ignorance and fear with gentle, compassionate, education and experience.

The last paragraph thrills me most. I indulge myself by reading it again. I already knew Charity had been a member of a panel set up in her department where people with different religious connections took different positions on the issue of homophobia. She'd told me about the vigorous and yet respectful debating and engagement with the student audience. Afterwards, she'd got an email from one of the 'anti'-debaters. He'd thought a lot since the panel. Many of her points really struck a chord with him. He'd asked for references to the studies she quoted, including some of the biblical information.

Just this week, Charity writes somewhat breathlessly, she'd heard more of how his journey was progressing. Skye, setting up a similar debate at a youth conference, phoned this same minister to see if he'd represent the 'anti' view in the discussion. He'd replied apologising that he couldn't, *because he had changed his mind.* Charity's italics leap off the page at me again. He is happy, she writes, to come to Skye's debate representing his current 'changed mind' position if they need that, but he couldn't speak the same way he had a year before.

I knew the minister concerned. He and I'd locked horns a few times in church debates. I wouldn't have picked he would ever change. I finger Charity's email and wonder how many people beside myself and Charity he'd heard or read and been influenced by. This guy, courageous enough to change his mind on this issue, is an example of an Early Majority person. His evolution will influence other Early Majority friends of his. It may even influence his acquaintances who remained in the Late Majority on this topic.

A quote from my evangelical past rolls round my brain. "No one gets a whole soul." It was a hoary old saying, but maybe the idea behind it was true in this context. No one person is ever solely responsible for another's change of heart. Large and small influencers each play a part. That includes the influence of the spirit. Grace always challenges our tendency to hide from confronting relationship behind walls of legal prohibitions.

Charity has come a long way on her journey to being a wholly realised human. She's evolved from the fearful, suicidal teenager I first met. She's become a confident young lesbian woman at home in her skin, nurtured by a relationship consistent with her sexual orientation. She's allowed negative experiences with her church to strengthen her resolve and educate her mind rather than crush or make her bitter. Now she is combining her very identity and inner being with her learning to assist others in her community to find their way in their place and their time.

It was highly probable that in her future, more meaning may indeed be found.

Thanks be given.

I drain my coffee cup and stretch out again in the lavender-laden air.

This is the end of Charity's beginning.

Glossary

Cis — A person who is content to live with the biological identity into which they are born.

Gay — A specific term for a homosexual man, but also used as a blanket term for both gay men and lesbian women.

Intersex — A person who may have been born with ambiguous genitalia or internal sex organs which contradict their outward appearance. Such people may have been assigned a sex at birth, by parents and/or medical personnel, which later does not feel right to the person.

Lesbian — A woman who is attracted sexually to other women.

Manse — House in which a minister lives, provided as part of their salary package by the church. In the Anglican tradition this is called a vicarage. In a Catholic tradition this is call the Presbytery.

Minister — Term for a clergyperson in mainstream churches.

Non-binary — A person who does not want to be thought of as either male or female, and takes on an identity which can be both or neither. A non-binary person would usually prefer the pronouns used to describe them to be 'they' or 'them' rather than 'he' or 'she.'

Ordained — When a minister or priest is officially approved by their church. Usually they are ordained to their first ministry position. After that, if they change churches the ceremony is called an 'induction.' In the Presbyterian tradition, lay people who serve as elders are also ordained.

Pastor	Term for a minister used in less formal churches such as Baptist and charismatic churches.
Priest	Term for a minister used in the Anglican and Catholic churches.
Queer	A word reclaimed from hate speech to be an umbrella term for gay men, lesbian women, bisexual persons and/or those using a non-binary identity.
Trans / Transgender	The prefix used for a person presenting initially as a man or a woman who changes their gender to the opposite, i.e. a trans woman is a male who has transitioned to being female, a trans man is a woman who has transitioned to being a male. Some may do this by dressing alone, others may have had hormone treatment which alters the body to some extent. Some may have had surgery to alter genitalia.
Vicar	Priest in charge of an Anglican church.

Appendix 1 – Recapturing the Flame

ARCC[117] worshipping together

Call to Worship

One:	Let us give thanks for God's steadfast love
All:	**For Godde's wonderful works towards humankind**
One:	Satisfying the thirsty
All:	**Filling the hungry with good things**
One:	God is with us
All:	**Godde's spirit is here**

Reading: Psalm 137[118]

One: We come together as a company of Christians wanting reconciliation between the heterosexual Christian community and those within the Church Community who are gay, lesbian, bisexual and transgendered.

All: **Along the journey thus far, there have been many moments of pain.**

One: Some moments have been those when the pain has been inflicted on us.

All: **At other times we have inflicted pain on ourselves.**

One: On other occasions pain has been inflicted by us onto others.

All: **Yet other times, the pain has been a collective wound of our whole church and society.**

One: Today we seek healing, forgiveness, a letting-go, even perhaps, just a brief moment when there is a cessation of hostilities.

All: **Whatever it is, we need right now.**
Whatever it is, we can accept right now.

One: We seek salve-ation – the salving of hurts inflicted, healing attention to raw wounds, healing of damage, sometimes unintentioned, but always real.

All: **Let us hear what God speaks**
For God will speak peace to God's people
To the faithful
To those who turn to God in their hearts
Surely God's salve-action is at hand. (Psalm 85).

One: On the pieces of paper you have been given
you are invited to write down
whatever it is you want to let go of,
Or to seek healing for,
Or to ask forgiveness for,
Or claim energy or comfort for,
Or to offer up.

Use this opportunity for what you need.

When you are ready,
bring your paper to be consumed in the fire,
so our journey to healing and wholeness
can be completed,
Or started,
Or continued for another step along the way.

[The papers are brought forward in silence]

Poem: *And so we must begin again* by Anna McKenzie[119]

[Silence]

We hear a story from the Hebrew tradition: Exodus 3:1-14.

[Silence]

Out of the midst of the hurt and the pain, some of which we have suffered and some of which we have caused, we have been able to light a candle flame. Out of the blackness of dusty ashes, out of the consuming fire, springs a new light for the way. "I am what I am," God promised Moses, or "God will be what God will be." The promise given to Moses was that the people of God would not be oppressed forever.

Let us recapture the light then, so we can continue our journey to the promised land of milk and honey, of freedom and joy. You each have a candle. You are invited to bring it forward, light it from the central candle and place it on one of the candlesticks to create our own burning bush of light and hope for the future.

If you cannot light your candle yet, please bring it unlit and place it with the others. The light can be carried for you by the group until you can recapture it for yourself again.

[The candles are placed and lit in silence]

> **One:** We have lit candles of hope, but the world we live in is still dark…let us pray in hope into that darkness.

For the darkness of waiting[120]

[Silence]

Jim Cotter's version of *The Lord's Prayer* said together[121]

Time to greet each other

Prayers for Ourselves and Others

> **One:** We have gathered with a sense of the sacredness
> of this place
> Of the spirit of life among us
> In our breathing, in our laughter,
> In our tears, our tiredness
> In our hopes and dreams as well as our fears,
> In the stillness.
> We know ourselves to be in the presence
> of the Holy One
> And the sacred earth, sea and sky embrace us.
> We come before Godde, made in God's image,
> Each of us a gift of life, in the quiet of this place.
>
> In the next space, we pray silently or aloud, for those much on our minds and for those who have asked us to pray for them

[Space for prayer]

Affirmation

One: Here is beauty, here is variety.
Each candle is different,
each flame unique and part of the whole.
We are beauty, we are variety.
Each person different,
each life unique and part of the whole.
Let us stand to affirm our faith in God and ourselves.

All **We are a cloth of diverse colours.**[122]

The Sharpness and Sweetness of God – a form of Eucharist[123]

[This form of Eucharist uses tart apples and sweet honey to express the mixture of feelings and experiences we encounter in life.]

Poem: *Resurrection* by Anna Gilkison

All: **Go with us into our life together**
As your ARCC people here in …..
Take all that we offer and add that to your gifts.
Breathe into our work your energy, truth and
courage, that we may be faithful, loving people
Truly gracious to each other
because we are truly committed
to the vision of life to which you call us.[124]

Song: *Fancy Noah sailing in the ark* (**Rainbow People**)
Lyrics and music by Colin Gibson[125]

Appendix 2 – Rainbow Resources

Still interested in church?

Even if you don't live in the cities where these churches are found, their websites can be great resources of affirming material. Since the Covid pandemic, more churches provide online worship services on their websites and Facebook pages.

MCC Church, Auckland, NZ and internationally

https://visitmccchurch.com/our-churches/

> "We welcome everyone. Find a MCC church. We are the gay church, LGBTQ church, human rights church & more. All are welcome. Queer friendly. Straight friendly."

The MCC church no longer meets in Auckland, though there are small groups meeting in South Auckland and Christchurch.

New Zealand churches which are inclusive and welcoming

Auckland

St Luke's Community, Remuera

https://stlukes.org.nz/contact/

> "The Community of St Luke affirms its commitment to being an inclusive, nurturing community where all may feel safe and accepted, free from coercion and judgmental attitudes.
>
> We especially want to emphasis this in light of the resolution passed by the Presbyterian National conference placing restrictions on people in de facto heterosexual or in gay or lesbian relationships. St Luke's dissented from that decision both in 2004 and in 2006. We look forward to seeing you and to you sharing with us in making a difference to people, society, and to the religious and spiritual quest through honest enquiry, good humour, warm compassion, commitment to diversity and openness to new perspectives."

St Matthews in the City
https://www.stmatthews.nz/

Auckland Rainbow Community Church has met every Sunday night at St Matthews for 45 years.
https://aucklandrainbowchurch.org

Gay and Christian group

"The Gay and Christian Discussion Group is an informal gay affirming discussion group that meets monthly to discuss issues that directly affect our faith, how we feel and what we can do for other Gay Christians. We DO NOT believe that being gay disqualifies anyone from living a full and faithful Christian life.

Our aim is to provide a safe forum for Christians who happen to be gay, lesbian, bisexual, or transgender to openly discuss their thoughts, hopes, and fears in a supportive and constructive environment without fear of instant condemnation. The group is open to people from all denominations, and any who are interested in finding out more about being gay and Christian. We are not limited to Ponsonby Baptist members. Our usual dates for meeting are the third Thursday of every month for an evening of Pizza and lively discussion. Contact us for details of upcoming discussion evenings or for more information."

Phone: 09 360 5595. Email: office@ponsonbybaptist.org.nz

http://www.ponsonbybaptist.org.nz/gay-and-christian-information.html

Wellington

St Andrew's on the Terrace
https://www.standrews.org.nz
An inner city Presbyterian church which has this notice on its façade, "Including all people of every creed, race, class and sexual orientation."

GalaXies meets informally at St Andrews every month
http://galaxies.org.nz/ and

https://www.facebook.com/galaxieswgtn/

Christchurch

Knox Church, Victoria Avenue
http://www.knoxchurch.co.nz/about.html

"Our Special Character:

Knox Church is a progressive congregation within the Presbyterian Church of Aotearoa New Zealand. We aim to create Christian community in which people of all ages, sexual orientations, cultural backgrounds and socio-economic situations are included as equally valued participants in our congregational life.

We cherish our diversity, offering a safe place of belonging to any who wish to explore their beliefs in an atmosphere promoting discussion, the development of healthy relationships and spiritual growth. We strive to be open to dialogue and shared experiences with people of other faiths.

We enjoy worshipping the God made known in Jesus, endeavouring to do so in ways that are relevant to our daily lives, respect the integrity of creation, and make a positive difference to our wider world."

Dunedin

Knox Church, 449 George Street
https://knoxchurch.net/

Opoho Presbyterian Church, Signal Hill Road, Opoho
https://www.opohochurch.org/

YouTube

English Vicar at Large, Dave Tomlinson offers a weekly YouTube, *The Holy Shed* which is wide ranging with progressive theology and a gay friendly vibe. Dave blessed his own daughter's marriage to a woman.

See especially https://youtu.be/GjKx4Dx3R-g which is entitled 'Finding Your Voice.'

Dave talks specifically about the rainbow community in other YouTube posts and writes about them affirmingly in *Black Sheep and Prodigals: An Antidote to Black and White Religion.* (Hodder, 2017).

Used to be a church goer, but don't understand or comprehend church anymore?

Books with an alternative view on how religion could be with a different perspective:

- *Wherever you are You are on the Journey.* Susan Jones (Philip Garside Publishing Ltd, Wellington, 2021).

- *Faith After Doubt: Why your beliefs stopped working and what to do about it.* Brian McLaren (St Martins Press, 2021).

- *Black Sheep and Prodigals: An Antidote to Black and White Religion.* Dave Tomlinson (Hodder, 2017).

Online Resources and Helplines

The website links listed in this section were current when this book was first published. Since then new websites may have launched and sites listed may have gone offline. A Google search will provide links to the latest New Zealand websites.

Feeling fragile?

Website of the NZ Mental Health Foundation lists national helplines (see below). https://mentalhealth.org.nz/helplines

National helplines

Need to talk? Free call or text 1737 any time for support from a trained counsellor. All the services listed here are available 24 hours a day, seven days a week unless otherwise specified.

- **Lifeline:** 0800-543-354 (0800 LIFELINE) or free text 4357 (HELP)

- **Suicide Crisis Helpline:** 0508-828-865 (0508 TAUTOKO)

- **Healthline:** 0800-611-116

- **Samaritans:** 0800-726-666

Helplines Brochure

A directory of helplines and local mental health service contact details can be downloaded from the Mental Health Foundation website:
https://mentalhealth.org.nz/resources/resource/helplines-and-local-mental-health-services

Depression-specific helplines

- **Depression Helpline:** 0800-111-757 or free text 4202, to talk to a trained counsellor about how you are feeling or to ask any questions.
  https://www.depression.org.nz/

  Includes the online self-help resource **Small Steps:**
  https://www.smallsteps.org.nz/

- **SPARX**
  https://www.sparx.org.nz/home

  Online e-therapy tool provided by the University of Auckland that helps young people learn skills to deal with feeling down, depressed or stressed.

Sexuality or gender identity helpline

- **OUTLine NZ:** 0800-688-5463 (OUTLINE)
  Provides confidential telephone support.

Non-binary or transgender or wondering if you are?

GenderMinorities: Non-binary and transgender support.
https://www.genderminorities.com/

"A nationwide transgender organisation. It is run by and for transgender people; including binary and non-binary, intersex, and irawhiti takatāpui. We support transgender people of all ages, cultures, and backgrounds, and provide one-to-one peer support and information nationwide."

Being Gay at school

InsideOUT

https://www.insideout.org.nz/

"InsideOUT works to give rainbow young people in Aotearoa New Zealand a sense of safety and belonging in their schools and communities.

We are a national charity providing resources, information, workshops, consulting and support for anything concerning rainbow or LGBTQIA+ issues and education for schools, workplaces and community organisations."

Comment on website:

"InsideOUT is really committed to including rangatahi voices within their work and creating positive experiences, and that value for my voice during my time with them has done wonders for my self-confidence."

Being young and gay

Rainbow Youth:

https://ry.org.nz/

"We work with young people, their whānau and their wider communities to provide safe and respectful support."

Intersex or Transgender

Intersex Trust Aotearoa New Zealand

https://www.ianz.org.nz/

"ITANZ is a New Zealand registered charitable trust and provides information, education and training for organisations and professionals who provide services to intersex people and their families."

For parents of gay, non-binary, transgender, rainbow children

Let's Talk: A Resource Guide for Parents – OutLine Aotearoa

https://outline.org.nz/parents/

"It is natural for parents to make assumptions about our children... If it's hard for you to accept the idea that your child might be gay or transgender, here are resources that may help."

For Parents of trans children

NZ Parents and Guardians of Transgender and Gender Diverse Children:
https://www.transgenderchildren.nz/

> "A parent-led group where you can find the information, guidance, advice and companionship to help you and your family safely and happily navigate your journey, knowing you are never alone."

New Zealand Family Planning

Provides advice and education for parents.
https://www.familyplanning.org.nz/advice/parents-and-carers/parenting-sexual-orientation-and-gender-identity

Appendix 3 – Reflections from Pride and Trans-themed services

Celebrating the 30ᵗʰ Anniversary of Homosexual Law Reform – Sunday 3 July 2016

Readings for the Gathering

1 Samuel 20:12-17: Then Jonathan said to David, "I swear by the God of Israel, that I will surely sound out my father by this time the day after tomorrow! If he is favourably disposed toward you, will I not send you word and let you know? But if my father intends to harm you, may Yahweh deal with Jonathan, be it ever so severely, if I do not let you know and send you away in peace. May Yahweh be with you as he has been with my father. But show me unfailing kindness like God's kindness as long as I live, so that I may not be killed, and do not ever cut off your kindness from my family – not even when Yahweh has cut off every one of David's enemies from the face of the earth." So Jonathan made a covenant with the house of David, saying, "May the LORD call David's enemies to account." And Jonathan had David reaffirm his oath out of love for him, because he loved him as he loved himself.

John 13:33-35: Jesus said to his disciples: "My children, I will be with you only a little longer. You will look for me, and just as I told the Jews, so I tell you now: Where I am going, you cannot come." "A new command I give you: Love one another. As I have loved you, so you must love one another. By this everyone will know that you are my disciples, if you love one another."

Contemporary reading from *Songs from the Midst of the Flames*, by David J Bromell, (Colcom Press, NZ, 1995) p. 75.

Breaking the silence is the first and hardest step. Stand up; stand tall; stand together. My hope is that Christian churches will yet become places where it is possible to speak our truth, including the truth of sexual abuse, harassment and homophobia, and receive respect and support. Where the concerns of individuals are owned by the community. Where men can listen to and respect the concerns of women, and act in solidarity with women. Where, too, space is made for men to re-discover an authentic male identity and masculine spirituality. Where being confronted by a sister's or a brother's pain opens a door to wholeness for all. Where change agents are embraced by the community, instead of being banished from it, so that their vision and energy for change is balanced by the wisdom that is consensus. Where justice, healing and peace can be created. Then we will be a sanctuary, a place of refuge, and a symbol of hope to a society that hasn't even begun to handle sexuality well.

Reflection for the Gathering

I have an eerie feeling of standing in a line of great people of courage and determination. Fran Wilde calls it 'standing on the shoulders of giants' – we'll hear her message later. The line goes back more than 30 years.

David and Jonathan's pledge of love and loyalty comes to us from around 1011 BCE, over 3000 years ago. Fifty years before (approximately) Saul had become the first king of ancient Israel but his reign went sour – without even a referendum on Brexit to spoil it! Shockingly, David was anointed before Saul had resigned, abdicated or died, so he is the young pretender. Jonathan is actually pledging and asking for undying loyalty from the one who will eventually unseat his father. Boris Johnson and Michael Gove couldn't have done better!

The pairing 'David and Jonathan' has slipped into our western culture – as well-known as 'horse and carriage' or 'Morecombe and Wise' or 'ben and jono' or 'Lady and Gaga' depending on your generation. It depends on the culture in which you move whether this undeniably passionate declaration of love is read as two men expressing the 'mateship' which soldiers or rugby players act on in valorous moments or whether we see here two gay or bisexual men falling in love at an extremely inconvenient moment.

In my family of origin, the first interpretation of 'especially good mates' was the answer! In the circles I move in now, the latter is a definite possibility, for some a foregone conclusion. The story of David has become myth and legend. We do not know how true it is on the outside, but for some truth rings on the inside. We cannot know objectively what this relationship was, but the heart can feel truth though facts are missing.

'David and Jonathan' for me evokes 'Martin and Ian,' dear friends I met in Dunedin in the 90s, when training for the ministry. It was fascinating to hear them tell of their first tentative beginnings in the 1970s when they were at risk of criminal proceedings should they be charged. First a young man working in radio, the other beginning in interior design, they later ran a coffee shop in Roslyn where blue-rinse matrons loved to go. They openly supported Rev David Bromell at Glenavon Methodist church in Dunedin and created a safe place in that little church for gay women and men. They founded P-Flag in Dunedin for parents of lesbians and gays and were so keen that high school aged gay guys and girls had a safer place to meet than they had had, they later began a gay youth group on Friday nights. Roger and I helped with that in its early days – a fascinating experience.

No civil union or marriage, but when Martin died in 2012, they must have been together for over 40 years. Their dinner parties were legendary – Ian producing marvellous food and both entertaining among Martin's beautiful interiors where he later might play piano duets or for a singalong. Generous, passionate and compassionate, wonderful role models. When I hear people suggesting all sorts of things about the gay community, I would think of Martin and Ian and grimace at the comparison. Other examples will come to your mind, of gay men and women who are 'ordinary people living their ordinary lives,' as Fran puts it.

1000 years after David and Jonathan, Jesus introduced a 'new commandment.' In the snippet Bill read from the book we call John's Gospel, Jesus urges his followers to love each other. He argues the mark of a Jesus follower *is* the love they show. Though the church likes to think of itself as a bunch of Jesus followers, we certainly don't always get this loving thing right.

I want to say today to all who have been hurt, rejected or damaged by stuff so-called Christians have said and done, or allowed to be said or done that I am profoundly sorry that happened to you. I apologise unreservedly that our Christian message has been so skewed and distorted. It should not have happened. It should not happen in the future.

Thirty years ago a coalition of Christians and others bravely achieved the passing of the Homosexual Law Reform Bill. They were opposed by others and by people who called themselves Christians too. Nine years later, David Bromell, fighting his own fight to be able to minister, moving from the Baptist church to the Methodist, finding the road proverbially tough, wrote the words of our contemporary reading. Twenty one years later we in the church have not achieved the state he calls for yet, church wide, "...a sanctuary, a place of refuge, and a symbol of hope..." though here we try to achieve that as consistently as we can within the institution.

As a community St Andrew's has worked hard to try and stop discrimination and abuse of LGBTQI communities – sometimes by being vocal, sometimes by acting, sometimes by strategizing in playing a waiting game. I am profoundly grateful to be here, privileged to stand on the shoulders of giants such as Rev. John Murray (who invited me to a hui at Ohope on this topic in 1990), and Rev. Dr Margaret Mayman who bravely stood and spoke at many a national church conference, demanding and getting respect from those who opposed her. I am sure she will speak out as clearly in Australia as the same issues are debated.

Here at St Andrew's we will keep on working to achieve that state which Jesus called the Kingdom of God where all are treated justly and where Love is the rule of law.

How you read the signs of the times depends in what culture you plant your feet. Some with feet firmly planted in heterosexual culture feel enough gains have been made. Others standing in a different place see otherwise. From where we stand, we can see there is more work to be done. We will do it.

Rev Dr Susan Jones

Message from Dame Fran Wilde for the occasion[126]

Thirty years these days isn't even half a lifetime – but it seems more than a lifetime since the gay law reform legislation went through Parliament.

This is an occasion to celebrate and to thank those who supported it. I recall vividly the hateful stereotypes and prejudice of many who led the opposition to the legislation. Their campaign reached a turning point when they presented the infamous petition to Parliament. With flags, religious and martial music and uniforms, the spectacle stirred something in many ordinary kiwis, and murmurings of comparisons with pre-war Germany were evident. People realised that the vilification and hatred which had been evident from some quarters did not represent the values that most New Zealanders wanted in our country.

The legislative campaign was the culmination of work by many people over a long period of time, reaching back to the early part of the twentieth century. Those of us who were active in it truly stood on the shoulders of giants – thoughtful people who had espoused the concept of tolerance when society had not yet experienced the significant social changes that were rolling through in the sixties, seventies and eighties. They included both gay and heterosexual people, from all walks of life, including religious people. We must recall and applaud their commitment.

In the same vein, I want to salute all the gay men who heeded the call for visibility during the parliamentary campaign in 1985 and 1986. The campaign was basically a public education outreach, providing information to the community and challenging stereotypes in the hope that people would, in turn, give their MPs permission to vote for the bill. Visibility of gay men was critical to demonstrate that they were just ordinary people leading ordinary lives, but under the cloud of criminality if they exercised their sexual preference. Visibility lifted the shroud of secrecy and people all over the country discovered that their workmate, friend, brother or son was gay – and was not a perverted child molester. Had the legislation failed, these brave men would have been even more persecuted, so the risk was high for them.

My thanks also go today to the people of Wellington who generally were staunch and supportive of the legislation and gave me and my children immense personal support during a difficult time.

Today as we celebrate the fact that our society has changed immensely in the last three decades, we should bear in mind that in Aotearoa New Zealand there is still a vein of conservative prejudice against the LGBT community. Young LGBT people, in particular, are highly vulnerable at a time when teenage-hood has enough intrinsic difficulties. We know there is bullying and we know that families need help in accepting their kids may be different from what they expected. Congregations such as St Andrews have a reputation for reaching out. May you continue in this way, helping to improve our community for future generations.

━━━━◆━━━━

Transgender Sunday of Remembrance – Sunday 19 November 2017

Readings for the Gathering

Isaiah 56:1-8: This is what God says: "Maintain justice and do what is right, for my salvation is close at hand and my righteousness will soon be revealed. Blessed is the one who does this – the person who holds it fast, who keeps the Sabbath and their hands from doing any evil." Let no foreigner who is bound to God say, "The God will surely exclude me." And let no eunuch complain, "I am only a dry tree." For this is what God says: "To the eunuchs who keep my Sabbaths, who choose what pleases me and hold fast to my covenant – to them I will give within my temple and its walls a memorial and a name better than sons and daughters; I will give them an everlasting name that will endure forever. And foreigners who bind themselves to God to minister to the divine, to love God's name and serve, all who keep the Sabbath without desecrating it and who hold fast to my covenant – these I will bring to my holy mountain and give them joy in my house of prayer. Their burnt offerings and sacrifices will be accepted on my altar; for my house will be called a house of prayer for all people." The Sovereign God declares – the one who gathers the exiles of Israel: "I will gather still others to them besides those already gathered."

Ecclesiastes 3:1-8 A Time for Everything:

There is a time for everything, and a season for every activity under the heavens:

a time to be born and a time to die,
a time to plant and a time to uproot,
a time to kill and a time to heal,
a time to tear down and a time to build,
a time to weep and a time to laugh,
a time to mourn and a time to dance,
a time to scatter stones and a time to gather them,
a time to embrace and a time to refrain from embracing,
a time to search and a time to give up,
a time to keep and a time to throw away,
a time to tear and a time to mend,
a time to be silent and a time to speak,
a time to love and a time to hate,
a time for war and a time for peace.

Luke 4:14-21 Jesus Rejected at Nazareth

Jesus returned to Galilee in the power of the Spirit, and news about him spread through the whole countryside. He was teaching in their synagogues, and everyone praised him. He went to Nazareth, where he had been brought up, and on the Sabbath day he went into the synagogue, as was his custom. He stood up to read, and the scroll of the prophet Isaiah was handed to him. Unrolling it, he found the place where it is written:

> "The Spirit of God is on me
> because I have been anointed
> to proclaim good news to the poor.
> God has sent me to proclaim freedom for the prisoners
> and recovery of sight for the blind,
> to set the oppressed free,
> to proclaim the year of God's favour."

Then he rolled up the scroll, gave it back to the attendant and sat down. The eyes of everyone in the synagogue were fastened on him. He began by saying to them, "Today this scripture is fulfilled in your hearing."

Contemporary reading: *To the Transgender Suicides,*
by Graff1980, 2015. H*llo Poetry.

You will never know
The peace of acceptance
Once you are finished
Put to earth
Life was harsher than the dirt
Parents made you feel worthless
Cause you wanted to wear a short dress
Because you felt different
Cut off
Disowned
Disavowed
One friend after another disappears
And no one hears
The sobs
No one feels the salty tears
No one holds your hands
Or offers you a hug

You were damned
By the those who demand
You conform
Where there was no warmth
The clock cuts you bitterly
Condemning you to be lonely
And I cry all the more
Knowing you won't be the only one
Not the only daughter wanting to be a son
Not the only male that wants to be female
Not the only soft face harden
Or hard face softened till the sorrow overflows
Till everyone you know closes the door
And you disappear forever more[127]

Reflection for the Gathering

It is not an easy thing to read the list of names provided for tomorrow's Transgender Day of Remembrance. We have sanitized the experience for you by reading out the names of the countries and the numbers listed as murdered or having taken their own lives. I am not sure we should have done that, but if we are honest, truly honest, how many of you or us would want to listen to 230 names along with the cause of death ranging from 'shot in the back' to 'run over by a vehicle' to 'tortured and beaten.' The full list is here should you want to read it and you can access the list on the TDOR website too.

It was a shock to me to realise that I was equally shocked last year when the number of names we could access was only in the eighties, we read them all out then, you might remember, in groups of ten, but still we spared you the causes of death, equally horrific. Yet, in the intervening year I had forgotten that sense of shock. It is just as well we remember each year.

As you listen to the countries being read out later, notice that Brazil whose tourism in part depends on mardi gras and samba parades, with their drag queens and transvestites, has the highest number of transgender casualties – 151. The US, bastion of freedom and equality, has 24 deaths listed, Mexico 47. I am left to wonder if these are true numbers and whether there are more unreported in other countries which report only 1 or 2 or 5.

Reading the list of actual causes of death leaves me wondering why so brutal a reaction, and why a majority of male-to-female trans victims?

It saddens me as a female to read that transphobia and homophobia have their deep roots in misogyny – in a deep-seated fear of and disrespect of the Feminine. This is why so many trans victims are in male-to-female transition. It is why the hate speech so often used of gay men has feminine overtones. By those who commit these terrible crimes it is seen as an indignity for men to become women or to act like women (at least that is how those phobic members of the population see it).

Crime against transgendered members of society is not an isolated or specific accident, nor is homophobia against both the gay and lesbian communities. It is not specialized only to these three groups, though they get a worse time in many places than women do. It is crime which arises from our society's skewed view of the Feminine, something which unfortunately mainstream Christianity has aided and abetted. Every male and every woman has a feminine side and a masculine side. All people are both feminine and masculine in our characteristics, yet in Western society the male is more valued. So men hide their feminine side (don't be a girl) and women who show too many masculine qualities are put down as 'too bossy.'

This is not a Christian nor a Jewish attitude. In the reading from Isaiah we hear the voice of God being employed to give a valued place to eunuchs and to foreigners/strangers, and at the end of the reading we heard "The Sovereign God declares – the one who gathers the exiles of Israel: "I will gather **still others** to them besides those already gathered."

Along with the chosen people of Israel in this passage the Sovereign God is also allowing in, welcoming in others who are different, including those whose bodies are different from the usual male model. And in the well-known Ecclesiastes reading, there is no dualist choice having to be made between two alternatives, seen as the one being 'good' and the other 'bad.' Here there is a time for everything and a rhythm for each activity.

Then centuries later when Jesus turns up at his local synagogue, the passage he is given to read he claims for his own – he is the one to release those in bondage of different kinds and to help those blinded by their own prejudice to see clearly and, as well, to free those who are oppressed.

Even when repressive scriptures are emphasized by those who are frightened and prejudiced, there are these passages proclaiming freedom, release and enlightenment in these ancient scriptures.

It is unfortunate, no, more than that, tragic, that the patriarchal society of the ancient scriptures has been assumed by our own times to be the biblical, holy norm – that suppression and repression of the Feminine is a thing to be desired. Not so. Yet, God has been traditionally referred to as always male, even the Holy Spirit which is most often pictured as a bird and whose name in Hebrew is feminine and in Greek is neuter, is referred to as he. Yet, this is not so, there are many feminine terms used in less well-known passages for the person called God in the Bible.

If you live in a world where the God of the universe is only thought of as male, that not only gives every male on earth permission to be king of the castle, it also tells each woman on earth that she is second best. No one even has to proclaim this, the metaphors do it silently. Just as when a country has a bully for a President, other citizens of the country feel they can bully others too, a male-only divinity spells out a certain worldview. Yet this is not the biblical position. God is mother and father, crone and king, guiding shepherd and mothering hen.

And what's more, either-or, good-bad, black-white, male-female, straight-gay, cis-trans are not Jewish or Christian dualisms. They are ancient Persian ideas, picked up by the Greeks along the way; employed because they are so useful for the group which thinks itself superior to maintain power and control over the group they see as inferior.

As we saw in the world wars, you can only torture a person if you have decided they are a non-person. You can only beat them to death if they have no value for you. You can hit and kill and maim and gas when the person in front of you is only for you an object on to which you can project all your fear of difference and otherness.

So, let me say this clearly to us all here today.

This is not the truly Christian way.

So many of us and our sister and brother Christians have been and are mistaken. Every person is equally valuable and loved.

> Men *and* women
> Straight *and* Gay
> Gay *and* Lesbian
> Cis *and* trans *and*
> those who choose not to define themselves by gender at all.

> Those who are settled and those in transition.

As in Ecclesiastes, there is a time and a place for all of us.

> Let us make sure we celebrate the Feminine –
> the creativity and colour associated with her,
> the softness and fertility she carries with her,
> the wisdom which Sophia uses as her strength.

> Let us celebrate women's power alongside male might;
> let us celebrate girls, especially when they become
> Prime Ministers!

That's what we can do externally.

But more importantly, inside ourselves, let us all, male and female, straight and gay, cis and trans, let us all allow the Feminine to teach us and guide us into all truth; the truth in which we can live and move and have our being without fear; a truth which is soft and firm, hard and gentle, fertile and freeing, creative and earthy, growing and celebrating.

Then we will all be free, as Jesus intended us to be, enjoying the freedom which he died proclaiming and protecting to the end.

And let us commit ourselves to remembering that real people become real victims when we do not honour the Feminine, in our own lives, in our churches and in our society.

Let us honour Her so one great day there will be no more deaths to commemorate but only life to celebrate.

So may it be.

Rev Dr Susan Jones

Pride Festival Week – Sunday 25 February 2018

Readings for the Gathering

Romans 4. (The Living Bible)

Abraham was, humanly speaking, the founder of our Jewish nation. What were his experiences concerning this question of being saved by faith? Was it because of his good deeds that God accepted him? If so, then he would have something to boast about. But from God's point of view Abraham had no basis at all for pride. For the Scriptures tell us Abraham *believed God*, and that is why God … declared him "not guilty."

But didn't he earn his right to heaven by all the good things he did? No, for being saved is a gift; if a person could earn it by being good, then it wouldn't be free – but it is! It is *given* to those who do *not* work for it. For God declares sinners to be good if they have faith in Christ to save them from God…

Now then, the question: Is this blessing given only to those who have faith in Christ but also keep the Jewish laws, or is the blessing also given to those who do not keep the Jewish rules but only trust in Christ? Well, what about Abraham? We say that he received these blessings through his faith. Was it by faith alone, or because he also kept the Jewish rules?

For the answer to that question, answer this one: *When* did God give this blessing to Abraham? **It was *before he became a Jew* – before he went through the Jewish initiation ceremony of circumcision.**

It wasn't until later on, *after* God had promised to bless him *because of his faith*, that he was circumcised. The circumcision ceremony was a sign that Abraham already had faith and that God had already accepted him and declared him just and good in his sight – before the ceremony took place. So Abraham is the spiritual father of those who believe and are saved without obeying Jewish laws.

Mark 8:31-38 (The Living Bible)

Then Jesus began to tell them about the terrible things he would suffer, and that he would be rejected by the elders and the chief priests and the other Jewish leaders – and be killed, and that he would rise again three days afterwards. He talked about it quite frankly with them, so Peter took him aside and chided him. "You shouldn't say things like that," he told Jesus.

Jesus turned and looked at his disciples and then said to Peter very sternly, "Satan, get behind me! You are looking at this only from a human point of view and not from God's."

Then he called his disciples and the crowds to come over and listen. "If any of you wants to be my follower," he told them, "you must put aside your own pleasures and shoulder your cross, and follow me closely. If you insist on saving your life, you will lose it. Only those who throw away their lives for my sake and for the sake of the Good News will ever know what it means to really live.

"And how does a man benefit if he gains the whole world and loses his soul in the process?

For is anything worth more than his soul?

**Contemporary Reading: 'Why I support Gay Marriage'
Interview with Tony Compolo.**

"I know all the arguments pro and con. I've thought of everything, and I'm still open to considering new things when somebody has something new to say. Having said all of that, I just meet too many wonderful Christian people who are in gay relationships, and I know this: my own marriage has been an incredible relationship. If I was to ask what has been the greatest influence in nurturing me as a Christian, I would have to say it's my wife. I then ask myself a very simple question: can I deny homosexual couples what I am personally experiencing in the way of blessings and joy in a relationship?

That became the basis for my final decision. I just knew too many couples who were living out the Christian life, who were committed to the work of the kingdom and who were in edifying relationships.

Suicide is the second major cause of death among teenagers in America, second only to automobile accidents. Almost three-quarters of those suicides are suicides by Christian young people who cannot reconcile their sexual orientation with what they're hearing from the pulpit. I don't know what the Church is about, but if it's about driving kids to suicide it's not doing the right thing."[128]

Reflection for the Gathering

We've talked about why we might go on a spiritual journey two weeks ago. Then we talked about what we need to pack for that journey. Today I want to expand on who makes the journey.

Recently I've been reflecting on the horrible tendency of our churches to exclude people who are 'other' than what some consider the 'norm'. In Pride Festival time, obviously my thoughts focused on the otherness of heterosexuality and gayness and the complexities of gender identities. One reaction to resist that, is for the whole 'religious/spirituality' thing to be softened and sanitised. We make it all about 'Loooove' and acceptance and 'don't worry about what that nasty old Bible says.'

And I have reflected that when I feel someone is rejecting *me*, it is not enough to be accepted by others whom I know are in my favour. I still wish that the original harsh rejector of my personhood could like me. That is the acceptance I crave.

So I pondered, if God has this popular and long standing reputation as harsh and nasty and judgmental, I might not want a kind of Disney-version-God to accept me, that would be too easy. I crave the acceptance of that old hoary judge on the throne of heaven.

I know today's Bible readings may have sounded strange to your ears therefore, if you have been hanging around the Disney style, 'keep it light' version of Christianity/Spirituality. But I think these two readings tell us that even that traditional God who is often portrayed as very finickity about who is 'in' and who is 'out,' has a wide, broad view.

In the first reading the author, Paul, was writing to the new Jesus followers who lived in Rome – a mix of Jews turned Jesus followers and non-Jews who were picking up on the Jesus Way. There have obviously been arguments in the Roman community about who is 'in' and who is 'out,' and what you need to do or be to be accepted by God. Do you have to first be a true son or daughter of Abraham, the father of the Jewish faith before being an OK follower of Jesus? Or, can you be accepted by this same God without the Jewish credential of circumcision. (You notice we are just dealing with male members of society here – presumably women had other problems being accepted but they are not dealt with here.)

Paul, who claims elsewhere to be the most 'Jewish of Jews' says something very surprising in reaction to these arguments. He points out that way, way back, millennia before, it was just Abraham and God. It was just Abraham and the call he felt came from God to move his family and livestock and household, lock, stock and nephew Lot from Haran high up there in Turkey to Israel. A huge journey especially on foot.

All Abraham did was follow that call deep inside him. As Paul puts it elsewhere in this chapter, at the time, there were no Jewish rules to follow! No ten commandments, no Leviticus (wouldn't **that** be nice!), no Deuteronomy telling you what to do with your harvest, no precise Passover instructions to follow. It was just Abraham, his God and trackless desert. Abe then, was accepted by God says Paul, because he trusted. Abraham. Was. Accepted. On. Trust.

Can we believe this? No confession of faith to subscribe to, no promises to make, no doctrine to learn, no tests of sexual orientation or gender identity. Just. Trust.

Often, we get hung up on whether or not we believe. We get confused about whether or not we have faith, especially enough faith or the right kind of faith. Here Paul is saying it is just important to trust the journey and the voice that calls you on it. (Quite a difficult thing I might add, for post-enlightenment people who are often hung up on doctrinal propositions and statements of faith in their various religious frameworks)

'Just' trusting of course is both sublimely simple and incredibly demanding at the same time. Trusting is precious and uncomplicated and widely accepting all at the same time as being the hardest thing you might even have done in your life.

As David Griebner says in his parable *The Carpenter and the Unbuilder*:

> "The important thing was simply to continue to put one foot in front of the other with love and trust."

Journeying and acceptance *is* profoundly simple. To be genuine, it also needs to be incredibly demanding. Peter, in the Gospel reading, fell into the trap we can sometimes fall into – the "keep-it-light" class of spiritual walkers. Jesus is being frank and honest about his premonition of how bad it was going to be for him when they got to Jerusalem. You didn't need to be supernatural to know that for Jesus to journey to Jerusalem at that particular time was the act of a lunatic. Peter is hating this portrayal of what could and, if Jesus is to be believed here, **would** happen. So he protests. He wants Jesus to stop talking in such a morbid fashion. Only, he is rocked back on his heels and called 'Satan' by his beloved Teacher. What?!!!

Jesus is suggesting strongly that seducing ourselves or others into taking the soft option is wrong, even, we could say, we would be doing something evil to our friend or colleague or newcomer to church. And that even if we were thinking to be kind and welcoming and accepting of anything and everything.

Members of the LGBTQI communities know that their journey in an often hostile world is hard; that there are phases of it you cannot miss out though you would like to. Acceptance and getting on to the journey is both simple *and* difficult.

Sometimes when the way is tough on our spiritual journeys, we can forget that we were simply accepted in the beginning without any credentials, without any good works or having to sign up to anything. We can mistake the difficulties we are facing for our own failures or for others' rejection. No, it is simply hard work. Incredibly rewarding, but hard work.

There is a kind of 'hard' like that, but there is also the *evil* kind of hard. Hard like the trend Tony Campolo rages about in the contemporary reading.

People in and outside churches who drive young people to suicide are dangerous people, like Peter. They are dangerous because they have not done their **own** hard work. That work is to learn to deal with their feelings towards others different from them. **They** are the deficient ones, not the rainbow people they are rejecting. They are unconscious of what they are doing. Jesus put it well on Good Friday when he asked for forgiveness for his persecutors because "they know not what they do."

This reading from Tony Campolo is startling because it is from Tony Campolo. Campolo is a well known evangelical speaker and writer in the States. Later in this same interview, he grieves that in changing his mind about rainbow issues, he has lost his former evangelical community. For them, the circle of rejects has grown from not only the gay community but also those who support them. Such is the blinkeredness of people who have not looked deeply within at their own phobias.

Jesus calls Peter to account for this; he calls us to account too.

We are accepted on trust onto the journey; but our journey will only be deep and true if we carry the cross we are **personally** meant to unpack and decipher and integrate into our lives.

For some, that cross is phobias about difference. For some the cross is our fear of rejection. For others our cross is our suspicion of religion and spirituality. There are many more crosses individuals have to encounter for themselves. What might your particular cross be this Lent?

This is all complex and deep and hard to explain. I hope I have managed to shed some light on its complexity, but also, part of this simple but difficult journey is working this out for yourself.

In the meantime, let's continue to accept each other on trust and let's put one foot in front of the other in love.

Rev Dr Susan Jones

Lent 1, Pride 1 – Sunday 10 March 2019

Readings for the Gathering

Hebrew Bible – Genesis 9:16

From the end of the Noah's ark story of the Great Flood

Whenever the **rainbow** appears in the clouds, I will see it and remember the everlasting covenant between God and all living creatures of every kind on the earth."

Ezekiel 1:28

From the account of the prophet Ezekiel's vision and call

Like the appearance of a rainbow in the clouds on a rainy day, so was the radiance around him. This was the appearance of the likeness of the glory of the LORD. When I saw it, I fell facedown, and I heard the voice of one speaking.

Gospel – Luke 4:1-13

The traditional reading for the first Sunday in Lent.

Jesus Is Tested in the Wilderness

Jesus, full of the Holy Spirit, left the Jordan and was led by the Spirit into the wilderness, where for forty days he was tempted by the devil. He ate nothing during those days, and at the end of them he was hungry. The devil said to him, "If you are the Son of God, tell this stone to become bread."

Jesus answered, "It is written: 'Humanity shall not live on bread alone.'"

The devil led him up to a high place and showed him in an instant all the kingdoms of the world. And the devil said to him, "I will give you all their authority and splendour; it has been given to me, and I can give it to anyone I want to. If you worship me, it will all be yours."

Jesus answered, "It is written: 'Worship the Lord your God and serve God only.'"

The devil led him to Jerusalem and had him stand on the highest point of the temple. "If you are the Son of God," the devil said, "throw yourself down from here. For it is written:

'God will command the angels concerning you to guard you carefully; they will lift you up in their hands, so that you will not strike your foot against a stone.'" Jesus answered, "It is said:

'Do not put the Lord your God to the test.'" When the all this tempting was finished the devil left him until an opportune time.

Contemporary Reading: 2016 Community Hero Awards, Australia. Community Hero Award winner – Rev Dorothy McRae-McMahon.

For over 30 years Dorothy has been a spiritual leader for LGBTI people and the LGBTI community and has championed acceptance and inclusion of LGBTI people in faith-based organisations. A peace activist in the 1960s, Dorothy was ordained a minister in the Uniting Church in 1982, leading the Pitt St congregation in Sydney and then taking on the role of National Director of Mission before becoming one of the first Uniting Church ministers to 'come out,' subsequently becoming a leader in the successful campaign to have homosexual ministers formally accepted within the Uniting Church, arguing that homosexuality was a sign of wholeness rather than evidence of moral decay. After retiring in 1997, [Dorothy] has remained engaged in ministry in an inner-Sydney Uniting Church, worked as co-editor of the *South Sydney Herald* and has continued to be recognised as an internationally renowned writer, liturgist and feminist theologian.[129]

Reflection for the Gathering

It has been my privilege to talk with quite a few gay and trans people about church and God and things like that. It might be on a phone call where the person calls to see if they would be welcome here. We talk for a while and sometimes the person turns up, other times they don't, at least at first. If you have had a few rebuffs, it is hard to try again. Often rainbow people who keep trying with the church have come from conservative backgrounds. The gift of the conservative Christianity they have known is that it has left them with a yearning to be loved and accepted by God and the strong need to know you are on a spiritual journey. The burden of such a background is that once you have become embedded in that ethos and that journey, on coming out to your congregation, you may find your former spiritual companions melt away into the mist, or worse, block your way on the road.

Some less conventional churches get the welcoming and accepting thing right. People within them, have moved to a place where they accept all people whatever or whoever they are without caring too much whether that is an orthodox position or not. Sometimes however, the God talked about in those churches, (or sometimes the God NOT talked about in those churches) isn't the same 'sound' God as a conservative gay Christians might be used to. I wonder whether that is a disappointment. Having got the impression from others that God rejects you, it would be nice if it was that exact same God who could accept you now. I have been pondering this. I think it is the same God to whom we relate both here and in other more conventional churches. It is not God that has changed or been reinvented, it is a different pair of spectacles put on by the beholder which makes the difference. We will get into the key disputed texts within the Bible next week, so let's put them aside for the moment and look at the general view of God we see in the Bible and as presented by the church.

The First Testament of the Bible is out of the Jewish religion. In this section of the Bible, a close relationship is forged between God and the tiny nation of Israel. They were located in one of the most disputed territories in the known world of the time. On the silk trade routes, Israel was hot property. Over the centuries it suffered wave upon wave of foreign occupation and control. Sometimes, if they were lucky, they got away with becoming a tributary of the current dominant empire, where they were left pretty much alone, (as long as they paid tribute each year). At other times, as when Jesus lived there, they were fully occupied and controlled by a foreign power such as Rome.

So, the concept of God being on our side was developed for an often oppressed and marginalised race. This was no dominant, established nuclear power, but a vulnerable group of generally subsistence farmers. Later the concept of God being 'on our side' was adopted by established Christendom – by the Holy Roman Empire – and later the British Empire, the Apartheid-supporting South African Government and even the Third Reich. *Then* the rhetoric of God is turned upside down – the rich and powerful claim 'dibs' with God. God slowly morphs into the protector of the elite acting as a judgmental, wrathful God towards those who break the establishment's rules.

In rebellion against this, particularly at the time in rebellion against the dominant collusion of the Roman Catholic church and South American governments, in the 1950s and 60s, a new pair of theological spectacles were being used by what came to be known as 'liberation theologians.' There was Gustavo Gutiérrez of Peru, Leonardo Boff of Brazil, Juan Luis Segundo of Uruguay, and Jon Sobrino of Spain. Together they popularized the phrase "Preferential option for the poor." The new pair of spectacles they had put on to read Scripture and do their theology was a marxist socio economic analysis – which critiqued the use of class and wealth to discriminate against the lower socio-economic levels of society. Liberation theology was the political *praxis* of Latin American theologians. As its name suggests, it liberated people who had been held under by churches, governments and theologians. It was not popular with the ruling authorities, as represented by Cardinal Ratzinger, who would become Pope Benedict. Boff was silenced by the church, and Gutierrez only fully reinstated with the Vatican in the last few years.

Praxis was an important word for these theologians – they critiqued strongly theology which was mere words and did not also carry with it care for the poor and action for social justice on a systemic scale. Liberation theologians pioneered the concept of putting on the spectacles of the context where you belong. Since, other liberation theologies have erupted and thrived – feminist theology looks at scriptures and God from a woman's perspective, womanist theology looks from a black woman's point of view. Black theology takes into account race. Rainbow theology takes into account sexual orientation and gender identity.

All these contextual theologies represent groups who have been marginalised from established society and often ill-treated within the conventional church – black and coloured communities, women, black women and the rainbow community. There are more.

This technique of reading the Gospels differently has sometimes been called looking at the Gospel from the underside. Same God, different spectacles on the noses of those reading the Scriptures and reading God.

There is an irony inherent in the morphing of the Christian view from the viewpoint of a vulnerable Israel to a dominant British Empire view of Scripture. In this change, the very critique of imperial use of force and might in Scripture has been turned on its head to in fact *endorse* such use of power and might.

As we have studied in the monthly study group, when early Christians used the phrase "Jesus is Lord" it was, at the time, a subversive political statement challenging the politically correct words "Caesar is Lord." When the theology of the Kingdom of God and the enthronement of Christ were developed it was in *contrast* to the kingdom of Caesar and the imperial throne of Rome. The use of 'Kingship' and 'Lord' in scripture was a critique and challenge to earthly power and control. Not that God was equally, if not more powerful, but that God's power was, in fact, as Jesus says to Pilate, "not of this world."

In a society which disrespects the rainbow community, both those of a different sexual orientation and those with changing gender identity, God is not on the side of the *disrespectors*, but on the side of the *disrespected*. Any who are oppressed marginalised, treated with prejudice and disdain, are the ones on whose side God is ranged.

When the majority take off their rose-coloured spectacles and put on their rainbow coloured spectacles, then they get a completely different view of the same God.

Following this line of sight, the wrath of God is quite properly directed at abusers, at homophobia, at prejudice and hate speech. So it shouldn't be a surprise that as far back as the prophet Ezekiel, hundreds of years before Jesus, Ezekiel's vision of God images the divine as brilliant and creative as a rainbow. *"Like the appearance of a **rainbow** in the clouds on a rainy day, so was the radiance around him. This was the appearance of the likeness of the glory of the* Lord.*"* When you think of a show of earthly glory it is usually the red and gold and purples which are used in coronations and crowns and regalia. If God, even the First Testament God, shows glory such as the rainbow shows, then softer blues and fresh young greens and everyday orange are also part of that glory. The flamboyant colours are part of the divine decorating scheme as well as the pastels and neutrals and quieter hues.

So it is with us. If you are discriminated against because of your orientation or gender preference, or if you have been abused, neglected or ill-treated, the divine is on your side. God did not condone or command your shame or ill treatment. God does not condone the wrong deeds of your detractors, just as God does not condone when you slip up. The message of scripture is that all are loved, all are welcomed at the gate to home, whoever they are and whatever they have done.

This week I have been doing a lot of funeral talk and it reminded me of a book I read about what happens when we die – I think it has relevance to how we live also. Here is a poetic form of the idea which caught my attention.

> The biblical myth has it that humankind
> was made out of the dust of the earth
> and then divine breath was breathed
> into that clay figure to bring it to life.
>
> At the end of life, that figure of clay,
> fashioned from the dust of the earth,
> is no longer the person we knew,
> and with respect,
> the empty body is sent to re-join
> the earth from whence it came.
>
> Departed from that clay body
> is the essential breath of life,
> which animated us and gave us vitality.
>
> The great myth of life tells us
> this one person's breath of life
> sprang from that original divine breath.
> In the act of death,
> it is freed to return home to its Source.
>
> So life's small breath joins indivisibly
> with the Breath of Life.
> And how could that breath
> be judged in any way since,
> as the myth tells us,
> that breath was first divine?[130]

These are big theological ideas, not historical facts I am talking about here.

We all have different bodies, different desires, motives, hormones, affections.

The biblical myth tells us those were created by God.

The biblical story tells us too that we are all animated by that divine breath, so we are all intimately one with the sacred.

Looking at this with rainbow spectacles, we can see that we are all different colours, which have all come from one Source of pure Light, refracted by our types and experiences and by the rain which falls into our lives into all the different hues and shades just as pure white light is refracted by the rain into the colours of the bow.

Our world is only complete when all the colours are present.

When will our church learn that it will only be complete when all colours are present?

Jesus refused in the desert to be tempted by the devil, to be arrogant about his own safety.

He refused to be controlled only by his physical desires.

He refused to accept a world where power and control were all his.

In those refusals he shows us the heart of God, to not lord it over the weak and powerless but, every time the rainbow appears in the clouds, to remember the everlasting covenant between the rainbow God and all living creatures of every kind on the earth.

Rev Dr Susan Jones

Appendix 4 – Saxophone Spirit

Saxophone Spirit

Where are you, God?

Are you
in the brief split second's hesitation
before the heart-catching moment
when the sax starts its sensual swirling sweep of sound
tingling down through her body
right from her cranium
to finally reach her toes

Was that moment of singing silence
that possession of singing sound
…you?

Where are you, God?

Are you in the brief split second's hesitation
before the heart-catching moment
when she trusts the gay woman in front of her
with her secret
that she too, is queer?
and the woman smiles
for she already knows

Where are you, God?

will there even be a brief, split second's hesitation
before you smile too
before she senses your joy filled presence
before in a heart catching moment
she knows
you are
that you are for her
what the church cannot be

For there is not even a brief, split second hesitation
before they,
those who want to keep it all the same
to live by three-century-old rules
when even today is out of date.
It will be no time at all
no time at all

before they will parrot out the old lines
"….hating sin…
but…
… loving sinner…."

And she knows
with no split-second hesitation
knows deep, deep within
In a heart catching moment
that they lie!

They lie
it is her they cannot tolerate
whether sinning or not
because…..?

Who knows?
The impulse is hardly Godly
but atavistically frightened
deep, deep within,
she is the ultimate threat,
the woman who does not need a man.

Are you there, God?

The throaty sax sound twists and turns and twists again,
It blows where it wills
and no-one knows how,
or where
it will breathe life and sound and sensuality next.

Are you here, God?
in the split second's silence
In the singing sound
In the sensuality of her being
in the orientation of life to which she has been brought.

the saxophone breathes into her soul,
blowing where it chooses.
She hears the sound of it
but does not know from when it comes
or whither it goes.

You are here God….
wind of love…
saxophone Spirit….
birthing from above!

Anon

Appendix 5 – Baby Thanksgiving and Naming

Because of the church's attitude towards the rainbow community, it was asked that this ceremony not refer to God. It does, however, provide a moment when the couple of women can be supported by their community, just as a congregation would support parents of a newly baptised child. It also gave them a chance to thank their friends and family for their support

Baby Thanksgiving and Naming
for a child and his lesbian mothers and donor father

Welcome

Thanksgiving for Yvette and Laura

> As we gather to give thanks for the gift of Cameron, we pause first to give thanks for the friendship and support which, as friends and family members, we have received from Yvette and Laura.
>
> For friendship and for fun filled times
> Simulating conversation and artistic talent

All: We give thanks

> For two personalities complementing each other
> Though as different as wavy hair and straight
> or as blonded hair and black

All: We give thanks

> For understanding and discretion
> For encouragement and hospitality received

All: We give thanks

> For a glimpse of what two lesbians can do
> Through their modelling of what love can be

All: For Yvette and Laura,
we give thanks
asking that their path ahead
be blessed with happiness and joy

Reading: *Of Children* by Kahlil Gibran

David is an integral part of the gifting of Cameron into our lives, Yvette and Laura bring him and Cameron to join them now.

Thanksgiving for the gift of Cameron

> For the excitement and exhilaration
> Of a newborn personality bursting into our lives

Parents: **We give thanks**

> For cheeky grin and wobbly legs
> For big blue eyes and curly hair

Parents: **We give thanks**

> For the joining of love and biology
> In a circle of women and man who parent this child
> Taking responsibility for his care

Parents: **We give thanks**

> For the potential of a new young human being
> Entrusted to us
> To shape and nurture and grow

Parents: **We give thanks**

> For the way in which our love is stretched
> to embrace another in the circle of our friendships

Parents: **We give thanks**
For all it means to have received
The gift of Cameron in our lives

The Naming

> What is the name of this child?

Parents: **Cameron Mark Caythorpe Wilson**

To Laura, Yvette and David

> Do you undertake to care for this child together to the best of your ability?

Parents **We do**

To the assembled multitude

> Do you undertake to support Yvette, Laura and David in whatever way you can best as they nurture this child?

People **We do**

Cameron Mark Caythorpe Wilson

You are welcome here amongst us
You are loved by three special parents who care for you deeply
and though you cannot yet tell us in words
we can tell you already know you are loved and wanted.

In different ways today we have undertaken to ensure that you
continue to experience love and care not only from your parents,
but through them, from us also.

The Blessing

Cameron Mark Caythorpe Wilson

May your life
be blessed with sunshine and shadow
with love and laughter

with tough times and good times
with all you need to grow to be:
generous of spirit and loving of soul.

Thanks in return

Laura and Yvette have requested that they have an opportunity to
return thanks to you all who have supported and cared for them in
many different ways.

	For support, understanding and acceptance as we chose to begin the process which has led to today
Laura & Yvette:	**We thank you**
	For the gift of life and for fatherly interest
Laura & Yvette:	**We thank you**
	For practical assistance both night and day for gifts and friendship For knowledge and conversations covering many a topic

Laura & Yvette:	**We thank you**
	For family support, babysitting, company, advice much needed and other kindnesses which spring to mind
Laura & Yvette:	**We thank you**
	For being here today as a symbol of the circle of your friendship and care for us and Cameron and for the loving welcome you have shown our son
Laura & Yvette:	**We thank you,** **Asking that the path ahead of you all** **Be blessed with happiness and joy**

Contemporary Reading: *I know a Rhino*

Later there will be time for people to speak in response should they wish to. To give think for you to think what you might day, we listen now to a selection of Cameron's musical favourites!

Some of Cameron's Favourite Animal Songs

Responses

The Rainbow of Love

Cameron's aunt brings to the front as a gift to Cameron, a rainbow candle to be lit on the anniversary of today or on his birthday (or both) to symbolise the multitudinous ways in which we as his community support and love him.

A Blessing said to each other as we go:

> **May you be enfolded in love**
> **Filled with peace**
> **And led in hope**
> **Through all your days Yes!**

This child turned 20 years old in 2022 and began flatting that year. On hearing his flatmates' descriptions of their family experiences, he told his two mothers that he had had the best parenting experience of the five of them.

Acknowledgements

Any book is influenced by many people and different threads of thought and debate.

I owe a debt to those I met in the church who saw both points of view, and those who advocated strongly, encountering hostility and risking their own advancement in the church and university.

I also thank those who led the church during these tumultuous years – mostly balancing the need for adherence-to-order with compassion for those becoming victims in the process. Duncan Jamieson stands out. I will not forget his communion at the end of the 1991 national church conference.

I can't properly estimate my debt to and admiration of the rainbow communities – outside and inside the church in Dunedin, Christchurch and Wellington especially. I have learned so much from courageous people, old and young, who knew their own deep truth and had the bravery to follow that despite its minority position in our church and society. I appreciate trust placed in me as they told their stories. I look at the increased freedom younger rainbow people have now and know it was hard won. I needed the push some of them gave – thank you, Jem Traylen. Thank you Christine Edwards for gifting me with glimpses of how life is for a lesbian woman and how differently life feels from a rainbow perspective.

Then there are other enlightened colleagues in mainstream denominations who spoke and advocated, called points of order and for secret ballots. I learned from them and appreciated our mutual support. Each time as a student minister, I called for a secret ballot in southern regional church meetings, one or two more votes were facilitated by that action. It taught me early on that this debate has made more than the rainbow community afraid to be themselves in the church.

David Gushee's *Changing our Mind* was a key book on my journey. In 2019, after the church refused a gift of 70 copies for study, I gave them away, hoping they'd be as helpful to those who took them.

Yvonne Wilkie and Trish Patrick have supported me through discussion and encouragement as well as 'reading duties.' Another, a younger lesbian woman, was also significantly foundational in shaping the book. The trigger warnings were her suggestion. Unfortunately, she prefers not to be identified – so the pain goes on. Reading this book was hard for her and others who identify as gay. It revived their anger at the church, so I doubly appreciate their help.

My husband Roger is an invaluable sounding board. He connects me with writing I would not otherwise have come across, like Jonathan Haidt, for example. He also shares my passion and compassion for those caught up in the negativity of this debate.

My publisher, Philip Garside, is the reason this book is in your hands. His commitment to publishing New Zealand books allied with spirituality and religion provides a publishing niche for this work. Philip's willingness to allow *Wherever you are, You are on the Journey* to multiply into a trilogy meant this book became a reality. His ordered, open-minded way of thinking has been vitally important. Thank you Philip.

Thank you, reader. Please allow yourself to learn from these pages. When you are done with them, if you trust the process, please tell others. Do recommend, gift or loan the book to those needing more information and encouragement to be authentic human beings whoever they are.

Gratefully,

Susan Jones

March 2022

Endnotes

1 Matthew 11:28-30, *The Message*.

2 'Recapturing the Flame,' Appendix 1.

3 https://www.psychologytoday.com/us/blog/the-time-cure/201801/the-trump-effect-update Accessed 18 March 2022. "Last spring we wrote a two-part post about "The Trump Effect," which was originally defined as an increase in bullying in schools caused by the rhetoric Donald Trump used during his presidential campaign. Now, a year into Mr. Trump's presidency, the definition of The Trump Effect has expanded to include religious and racial bullying by adults as well as: misogyny, sexual assault, and other socially unacceptable behaviors."

4 Jonathan Haidt, *The Righteous Mind: Why Good People Are Divided by Politics and Religion*, (Penguin Books, London, UK, 2013.)

5 https://www.ted.com/talks/jonathan_haidt_the_moral_roots_of_liberals_and_conservatives? Accessed 18 March 2022.

6 https://www.reuters.com/article/us-health-lgbq-religion-suicide-idUSKBN1HK2MA Accessed 18 March 2022.

7 https://psychiatry-training.wiki.otago.ac.nz/images/e/e7/Lucassen11.pdf Accessed 18 March 2022.

8 The movie *Pride* was released in 2014 but is set in 1984 during the British miners' strike. A group of lesbian and gay activists decide to raise money to support the families affected by the strike. The film shows what happens when the two groups meet and get to know one another.

9 https://www.britannica.com/topic/Christian-fundamentalism Accessed 18 March 2022.

10 *Joyeux Noel*, written and directed by Christian Carion, first screened at the 2005 Cannes Film Festival.

11 https://www.linkedin.com/pulse/technology-adoption-lifecycle-anastasiya-kaurdakova?trk=public_profile_article_view Accessed 18 March 2022.

12 When churches were not able to meet in person, many used Zoom and YouTube to communicate virtually and live stream services when lockdowns were in progress.

13 Published in 2017.

14 Published in 2020.

15 Brian McLaren is one of the leaders of the emergent church movement in the US. https://brianmclaren.net/

16 Google search 15 January 2022.

17 Google search 11 May 2021.

18 Luke 8: 1-3. *New International Version* (NIV).

19 David Tacey, *Religion as Metaphor: Beyond Literal Belief.* (Transaction Publishers New Brunswick (U.S.A.) & London (U.K.), 2015.) p. 25.

20 David P. Gushee, *Changing our Mind* (Read the Spirit Books, Michigan, USA, 2015) 2nd ed. pp. 56-7.

21 The full First Testament references are Genesis 1-2, Genesis 19, Leviticus 18:22-20:13 and Judges 19. The Second Testament passages Gushee analyses are Matthew 19:1-12, Mark 10:2-12, Romans 2:26-27, 1 Corinthians 6: 9, 1 Timothy1:10.

22 Eve and Adam: Genesis 2-3. Reread lecture by Phyllis Trible Copyright 1973 by Andover Newton Theological School. https://www.law.csuohio.edu/sites/default/files/shared/eve_and_adam-text_analysis-2.pdf Accessed 18 March 2022.

23 Trible, Phyllis, *Texts of Terror: Literary-Feminist Readings of Biblical Narratives* (Philadelphia, Fortress, 1984.)

24 Genesis 18:22-33. *New International Version* (NIV).

25 Gushee, *Changing our Mind*, p.61.

26 Ibid., pp. 61-62.

27 William Loader, *The New Testament on Sexuality* (Grand Rapids, William B. Eerdmans Publishing, 2012.)

28 Gushee, op. cit., p. 62

29 Ibid., p. 63.

30 Leviticus 18:22 and Leviticus 20:13. *New International Version* (NIV).

31 Leviticus 18:22 and Leviticus 20:13. *King James Version* (KJV).

32 Gushee, op. cit., p. 67

33 Ibid., p. 67.

34 https://www.americamagazine.org/faith/2010/08/18/dr-laura-and-leviticus Accessed 15 January 2022.

35 Susan Jones, November 2021.

36 https://www.forgeonline.org/blog/2019/3/8/what-about-romans-124-27 Accessed 18 March 2022 and https://pinkmantaray.com/bible Accessed 18 March 2022

37 'The German Invention of Homosexuality,' Robert Beachy, *The Journal of Modern History, Vol. 82, No. 4,* Science and the Making of Modern Culture (December 2010), pp. 801-838 (38 pages) (The University of Chicago Press.)

38 https://www.newyorker.com/magazine/2015/01/26/berlin-story This article suggests this was in the context of the 'invention' of gay rights in Berlin in the 19th century.

39 https://um-insight.net/perspectives/has-%E2%80%9Chomosexual%E2%80%9D-always-been-in-the-bible/ Interview with Ed Oxford: "Has 'Homosexual' always been in the Bible?" by The Forge Online, 14 October 2019. Accessed 18 March 2022.

40 Reddit – Open Christian https://tinyurl.com/26e2rw8s Posted by u/deegood 2020. Accessed 18 March 2022.

41 David Crumm: How 'Changing Our Mind' changed thousands of lives, starting with the author, posted on https://tinyurl.com/5xatemkf Accessed 18 March 2022.

42 Ibid.

43 Ibid.

44 Mark 2:27 *King James Version.*

45 John 10:10 *King James Version.*

46 *The Merchant of Venice,* (Act III, scene I), in *William Shakespeare: The Complete Works, Compact edition,* (Oxford, UK, Oxford University Press, 1988.) p. 438

47 Luke 6:31 *New International Version.*

48 Google search 12 August 2021.

49 Isaiah 1:17. *New International Version.*

50 Micah 6:8. *New International Version.*

51 John 8:6b-7 *New International Version.*

52 John 8:8-9 *New International Version.*

53 *Liberal and Conservative Representations of the Good Society: A (Social) Structural Topic Modeling Approach* by Joanna Sterling, John T. Jost, Curtis D. Hardin. First Published 3 May 2019. Sage Journals https://tinyurl.com/yc2xwnmf Accessed 18 March 2022.

54 Matthew 11 *King James Version.*

55 Matthew 11 *The Message.*

56 Google search September 2021.

57 Google search 12 February 2022.

58 https://en.wikipedia.org/wiki/Oppression Accessed 18 March 2022.

59 'Oppression and discrimination among lesbian, gay, bisexual, and Transgendered people and communities: a challenge for community psychology' By Gary W Harper, Margaret Schneider *American Journal of Community Psychology*. 2003 Jun; 31(3-4):243-52, p.243. https://pubmed.ncbi.nlm.nih.gov/12866682/ Accessed 18 March 2022.

60 'Brief reports: Unequal treatment: mental health care for sexual and gender minority groups in a rural state.' by Cathleen E Willging 1, Melina Salvador, Miria Kano, Psychiatric Services. 2006 Jun;57(6):867-70. https://pubmed.ncbi.nlm.nih.gov/16754766/ Accessed 18 March 2022.

61 https://www.massey.ac.nz/massey/about-massey/news/article.cfm?mnarticle_uuid=761A7828-96BF-57FE-AE21-2B460843F2FE Accessed 18 March 2022.

62 Ibid.

63 https://hail.to/laidlaw-college/publication/emCooni/article/lNWtAy4 Accessed 18 March 2022.

64 Ibid.

65 Ibid.

66 Italics mine.

67 'Long overdue': Government's $4 million funding for Rainbow community wellbeing 14 Feb, 2021 05:00 AM NZ Herald. https://tinyurl.com/2wpmxww9 Accessed 18 March 2022.

68 Mark Beehre, *A Queer Existence*, (Massey University Press, 2021).

69 *Nine to Noon*, Tuesday 28 September 2021. https://tinyurl.com/5h4cp6yn Accessed 18 March 2022.

70 https://www.stuff.co.nz/life-style/gender-and-society/127368266/violating-transgender-passenger-upset-by-patdown-or-nofly-call-at-wellington-airport Accessed 18 March 2022.

71 https://insideout.org.nz/ Accessed 18 March 2022.

72 https://www.insideout.org.nz/wp-content/uploads/2021/08/InsideOUT-rainbow-terminology-August-2021.pdf Accessed 18 March 2022.

73 Ibid., p. 10

74 Google search 22 August 2021.

75 https://www.stuff.co.nz/life-style/gender-and-society/125333190/queens-birthday-honours-intersex-advocate-mani-bruce-mitchell-on--doing-the-mahi Accessed 18 March 2022.

76 Ibid.

77 Ibid.

78 Rainbow terminology, InsideOUT website, op. cit., p. 8.

79 https://www.theguardian.com/world/2021/sep/15/new-zealand-bill-to-ban-lgbtq-conversion-practices-receives-record-100000-submissions Accessed 18 March 2022.

80 https://www.rnz.co.nz/news/political/451534/churches-at-odds-over-conversion-therapy-in-oral-submissions Accessed 18 March 2022.

81 Hansard. https://tinyurl.com/2ehh2wpv Accessed 18 March 2022.

82 https://www.rnz.co.nz/news/national/461599/politicians-react-as-bill-to-ban-conversion-therapy-passes Accessed 18 March 2022.

83 https://en.wikipedia.org/wiki/Conversion_therapy Accessed 18 March 2022.

84 Warren Wendel Wiersbe, often attributed to Mahatma Ghandi.

85 Written by Clare Herbert Woolston, (an Illinois preacher) in the late 1800s. The words were set to music by George Root using a Civil War marching tune.

86 https://en.wikipedia.org/wiki/List_of_gay,_lesbian_or_bisexual_people:_W%E2%80%93Z#cite_note-144 Accessed 18 March 2022.

87 "Hearing in NZ Murder of Boy, 14." PlanetOut. 19 October 1999. Archived from the original on 19 September 2003. Retrieved 13 June 2007. Accessed 27 September 2021.

88 Research archive, Victoria University, Wellington. https://tinyurl.com/yn5eer28 Accessed 18 March 2022.

89 https://www.nzherald.co.nz/entertainment/three-men-three-shows-joy-and-heartache-from-start-to-finn/TOXPE2JXSF6N5B6Y7EB2YP7I4Q/ Accessed 18 March 2022.

90 Later thought expressed in personal email to the author dated 23 August 2021.

91 https://morgancarpenter.com/intersex-flag/ Accessed 18 March 2022.

92 https://en.wikipedia.org/wiki/Eliana_Rubashkyn Accessed 18 March 2022.

93 https://en.wikipedia.org/wiki/Georgina_Beyer Accessed 18 March 2022.

94 https://www.theguardian.com/stage/2020/nov/05/richard-obrien-interview-rocky-horror-trans-crack-stroke-70s Accessed 18 March 2022.

95 https://www.youtube.com/watch?v=s_UbmaZQx74 This video gives an example of Peterson arguing his opposition to this. Accessed 18 March 2022.

96 https://thevarsity.ca/2016/10/03/u-of-t-community-responds-to-jordan-peterson-on-gender-identities/ Accessed 18 March 2022.

97 Alice Walker, *The Color Purple*, (U.S., Harcourt Brace Jovanich, San Diego, CA., 1982.)

98 Audre Lorde *Chosen Poems: Old and New.* (New York: W. W. Norton Publishing, 1982.)

99 Mary Oliver, *Devotions: The Selected Poems of Mary Oliver* (Penguin Press New York, NY, 2017.)

100 Paula Boock, *Truth Dare or Promise*, (Penguin Books, Auckland, NZ, 2013.)

101 https://youtu.be/VMUz2TNMvL0 Accessed 18 March 2022.

102 https://youtu.be/b5820mefpDM Janis Ian talks and sings about getting married. Accessed 18 March 2022.

103 Alice Walker, *The World has Changed: Conversations with Alice Walker* (The New Press, New York, NY., 2010.), p. 277.

104 Susan Jones, *Wherever you are, You are on the Journey* (Philip Garside Publishing Ltd, Wellington, 2021.)

105 1 Samuel 18 and into 2 Samuel. *New International Version* (NIV).

106 Ruth 1:16. *New International Version* (NIV).

107 In the 2021-2022 Advent/Christmas/Epiphany period. YouTube *The Holy Shed* Dave Tomlinson

108 See Appendix 3 for some of those reflections.

109 Alice Walker, *The World has Changed: Conversations with Alice Walker* (The New Press, New York, NY., 2010.) p. 277.)

110 Alice Walker, *The Color Purple* op.cit., pp. 176-177

111 *Officium* is a 1994 album by Norwegian saxophonist Jan Garbarek and early music vocal group Hilliard Ensemble ECM New Series. The piece which should accompany this poem is 'Parce mihi domine' (from the Officium Defunctorum by Cristóbal de Morales).

112 See Appendix 4

113 Line in the hymn 'We bring thankful hearts' written by Susan Jones to the tune Thaxted in *Progressing the Journey: Lyrics and Liturgy for a Conscious Church.* (Philip Garside Publishing Ltd, Wellington, 2022.)

114 https://www.royalsociety.org.nz/assets/Uploads/Our-futures-submissionPaul-Morris.pdf Accessed 18 March 2022.

115 https://www.youtube.com/watch?v=b5820mefpDM Accessed 18 March 2022.

116 See Appendix 5

117 ARCC stands for Association of Reconciling Christians and Churches. This was a local, informal grouping which gathered for this alternative worship.

118 David Grant, *Grant us your Peace.* (Chalice Press, Nashville TN., 1998).

119 Cited in Sheila Cassidy, *Good Friday People.* (Darton, Longman and Todd, London, UK., 1991.), p. 189.

120 Janet Morley, *All Desires Known,* 1st ed., (SPCK Publishing, London, UK., 2005).

121 *A New Zealand Prayer Book.* https://anglicanprayerbook.nz/

122 Dorothy McRae-McMahon, *The Glory of Blood, Sweat and tears: Liturgies for living and dying.*

123 June Boyce Tillman in *Human Rites*

124 Adapted from Dorothy McRae-McMahon op cit.

125 *Faith Forever Singing.* NZ Hymnbook Trust. (2000). https://pgpl.co.nz/new-zealand-hymnbook-trust-music-books-and-cds/

126 Dame Fran's message is reprinted with permission. For more information about her, see https://nzhistory.govt.nz/people/fran-wilde Accessed 18 March 2022.

127 Written by Graff1980, 2015. H*llo Poetry: https://hellopoetry.com/poem/1265008/to-the-transgender-suicides/ Accessed 18 March 2022.

128 https://www.premierchristianity.com/home/tony-campolo-why-gay-christians-should-be-fully-accepted-into-the-church/3423.article Accessed 18 March 2022.

129 https://youtu.be/B3R2UJcyirY Accessed 18 March 2022.

130 Susan Jones, with thanks for the concept to Penelope Wilcox, *The Hawk and the Dove.* (Crossway, Wheaton, IL., 2000).

Recent & forthcoming books by Susan Jones from Philip Garside Publishing Ltd

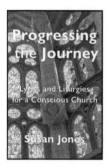

Progressing on the Journey:
Lyrics and liturgy for a conscious church

Words for 40 new hymns, that can be sung to well known tunes, which address contemporary issues and celebrate the church year.

This book also contains a wealth of responsive prayers and liturgy for worship.

Includes: Gatherings, Creeds, Affirmations, Communion liturgies, Blessings, poems and two Reflections.
(Print and eBooks now available.)

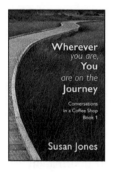

Wherever You Are, You Are On The Journey:
Conversations in a Coffee Shop Book 1

Do you feel there is more to Christian faith than is told on Sundays? Are you questioning whether the firmly held beliefs you grew up with are going to be useful in the next stage of your life?

Don't panic! You have simply reached a transition point in your faith journey.

Hope and her minister/mentor Susan chat about deepening & re-enchanting faith at their local café.

(Print and eBooks now available.)

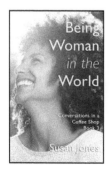

Being Woman in the World:
Conversations in a Coffee Shop Book 3

Faith's weekly coffee bar conversations with her minister explore the Feminine – in psychology and theology, women in biblical texts, roles in church and society, God and gender, women and spirituality. They cover the range!
(Print and eBooks publishing in 2022.)